"They call me Beanpole"

My mother says they call me names because they're jealous. She says that they all wish they were nice and tall and slender like I am. I used to believe her. But the older I get, the more I realize that mothers use that jealousy excuse for everything that comes along. I have a feeling that if I had only one leg and all the kids called me Peg Leg, my mother would say it was because they were jealous of how well I hopped.

BEANPOLE

BARBARA PARK

BULLSEYE BOOKS • ALFRED A. KNOPF
NEW YORK

Especially for Richard

Contents

1

Sticks and Stones

Grandma Woo-Woo says that life is full of disappointments. She says that just when it seems like you're sailing along smoothly, life will find a way to reach out and rock your boat. Sometimes, my grandmother can be a pretty depressing person. And I don't think I helped her spirits much by naming her Woo-Woo. She tried to get me to call her Grammie, but my mother said that when I was two, I called everyone Woo-Woo, and for some reason when it came to my grandmother, the name just stuck.

Personally, now that I'm almost thirteen, I wouldn't mind calling her Grammie. But changing names after thirteen years would just be too hard.

Besides, if I was going to change anyone's name, the first one to go would be my own. Lillian Iris Pinkerton. I still don't know how my mother could have done that to me. She says that she named me after her two favorite flowers, the lily of the valley, and the purple iris. I know she meant well, but I wish she'd been into animals instead of flowers when I was born. I'd much rather be called Fawn or Robin.

One time, we got into an argument about it, and I told her that if she wanted to name me after a plant, the least she could have done was pick a cute name like Holly, or Ginger. But my mother just chuckled and said I should be grateful her favorite flower wasn't a gladiola. Well, if you ask me, even Gladiola would have been better than Lillian Iris Pinkerton. At least that way, my initials wouldn't spell "lip."

Sometimes, though, I think that my grandmother is right about life's disappointments. For the first six years of my life, everything seemed to be going along perfectly. Mostly, I just ate and slept and colored. Then, wham! I hit the door of Mrs. Callahan's first-grade classroom, and my whole life fell apart. I wasn't inside the room for more than ten minutes before David Garbanzo sat down next to me and told me that Santa Claus and the tooth fairy had been in a big automobile accident, and they had both been killed. I was so upset at the news that I started crying and had to go to the nurse.

I spent the next few months avoiding David Garbanzo, and, for a while, I was back to smooth sailing again. But just when I was least expecting it, life reached out and rocked my boat again.

It was Valentine's Day. We had just finished our class party, and our teacher had started passing out the cards from the big valentine box in the front of the room. For days, I was sure that I would be the only kid in the class who wouldn't get a single valentine. In fact, I was so scared about it, I addressed two cards to myself, just in case no one else remembered me. Luckily, though, that didn't happen. I can still recall my excitement as the cards stacked up in front of me.

Anxious to find out who my many friends were, I ripped open the first envelope and laughed at the funny picture on the front. There were two cocker spaniels hugging each other, and it said: *Valentine, you sure look dog-gone good to me!* I turned it over right away to see who had sent it. And there, in thick black crayon, were the words *I LOVE YOU! your friend, Rolf Spangler.*

I thought I would die. Rolf Spangler sat right

behind me and was the jerkiest kid in the class. Rolf was the kind of kid who thinks it's funny to tap you on the shoulder and then pretend he didn't do it.

Quickly, I tried to stuff the card back in the envelope so no one else could see it. Suddenly, I felt someone tap me on the shoulder. Naturally, I knew it was Rolf. But as usual, when I turned around, he was sitting there pretending he was reading. He was grinning so hard, he drooled on one of the pages.

Disgusted, I turned back around and opened my next card. It was from David Garbanzo. He didn't sign his name, but on the back he had written, *P.S. The Easter Bunny shot himself,* so I knew right away it was him.

After that, I couldn't bring myself to open any more cards. Instead, I put them in my lunch box and took them home, where my mother accidentally threw them all away. I never did find out who all my many friends were.

When first grade was over, I thought I was ready for any disappointment life could hand me. After all, when you find out your secret admirer's a drooler, no problem seems too big to handle. But I was wrong. Suddenly my boat started rocking again, and it hasn't stopped yet.

The summer after first grade was the summer I started to grow. And unfortunately, out of all the things I've ever tried to do in my life, growing has turned out to be what I do best. It's stopping that's giving me problems.

I started shooting straight up that June. By the end of the second grade, I was almost two inches taller than anyone else in my class. And to make matters worse, I wasn't putting on much weight, so being skinny made me seem even taller. By the time third grade rolled around, I was so gawky, I was chosen to be the maypole in our school's spring pageant.

Instead of getting to dress up like a tulip or a rose like the other girls, I was wrapped from head to toe in brown paper and carried out to the middle of the stage. Then, when the curtain opened, about a thousand slobbering kindergarteners ran around tying me up with crepe-paper streamers. Except for the two eye holes, the only part of me showing was my nose. Even my feet were in brown paper bags.

At the end of the act, I was supposed to bow, but I was afraid if I bent over I would fall down, so I just stood there hoping that no one would recognize my nose. But as it turned out, everyone already knew who I was. It was in the pageant program:

MRS. BLUE JAY ....Cindy Walker
MR. SUN ....Danny Adams

7

The school pageant was over five years ago, but there's still a girl in my class who calls me Maypole. The rest of them have switched to Beanpole. It was a name given to me by Katrina Miller's mother. Katrina was a friend of mine at the time, and once when we were having a big fight, she told me that her mother felt sorry for me because I was such a beanpole.

"Oh, yeah? Well, I'd much rather be a beanpole than look like you do, Katrina. *My* mother says that you have legs like tree trunks," I lied. "So why don't you have your mom go plant you in the forest somewhere?"

Katrina started crying. She was one of those kids who could dish it out but couldn't take it. Mrs. Miller sent me home. She said it wasn't nice to make fun of someone else's trunks. She had meant to say legs, but she was so mad she got mixed up. It sounded so funny, I laughed all the way home.

When I got there, I pulled out our big family dictionary and looked up the word *beanpole*. Anytime you're called a name, it's usually interesting to look it up. But in the case of beanpole, it didn't turn out to be interesting at all. It meant exactly what it

8

sounded like: "**beanpole** (bēn′ pōl′) *n.* 1: a tall pole for a bean plant to climb on. 2: *Informal.* a tall, lanky person."

Anyway, Katrina never got over being mad at me and started calling me Beanpole at school. It wasn't long before everyone else was doing the same thing. I tried to get them to call Katrina Old Tree Trunk Legs, but it didn't catch on. I think a mean name has to be short, or kids forget it.

My mother says they call me names because they're jealous. She says that they all wish they were nice and tall and slender like I am. I used to believe her. But the older I get, the more I realize that mothers use that jealousy excuse for everything that comes along. I have a feeling that if I only had one leg and all the kids called me Peg Leg, my mother would say it was because they were jealous of how well I hopped.

My mother also spends a lot of time telling me that sticks and stones can break my bones, but names can never hurt me. She's wrong about that, too. Names *can* hurt me. I'd much rather be hit with a stick than be called a beanpole. A stick or a stone only stings for a minute. A name seems to hurt forever.

Let's face it, kids know a lot more about name-calling than parents do. So far—in addition to Beanpole—I've been called everything from Giraffe Legs to Olive Oyl. Last year, Ricky Hartman said he had a great new game, and he asked me to stand sideways and stick out my tongue. Being a good sport, I followed his directions. That's when he pointed and said I looked like a zipper. Luckily, I got to the girls' room before I started crying.

I suppose that when you look at people long enough, everyone has something about themselves they don't like. My mother thinks her eyes are too small, and my dad says his hands are too big for his body. Still, most people can hide the things they don't like about themselves a lot easier than I can. For example, my mother can wear dark glasses to hide her eyes, and my dad can walk around with his big hands in his pockets. But the only way I can cover up my height is by throwing a sheet over my head, and then I end up looking like a floor lamp.

Once, when I was really feeling upset, Grandma Woo-Woo tried to make me feel better by telling me the story of the ugly duckling. Some help. The name alone made me sick. She kept saying, "Don't you see, Lillian? It was the awkward, ugly one who grew to be the beautiful, graceful swan." It didn't make me feel better, though. It only made me hate ducks.

Right now, I'm five feet six inches tall. My mother's only five feet four, and my dad's only five nine. For a long time, I thought I was adopted. For months, I really drove my parents crazy. I told them it was plain to see that I didn't belong to them, so they might as well admit it. I was convinced that my real mother and father were probably with the circus doing some kind of "tall" act.

My poor mother did everything she could to convince me that I was hers. She even showed me pictures of her when she was pregnant. It didn't work, though. I told her she was probably just overweight.

It wasn't until we started having sex education classes at school that I finally got the message. My teacher, Mrs. Murray, explained that the children in a family look the way they do because of certain "genes" that are passed on to them by their parents. As soon as Mrs. Murray said "genes," Kathy Patterson raised her hand.

"What if your mother never wore jeans?" she asked, trying to keep herself from laughing.

The whole class cracked up. Even Mrs. Murray smiled a little.

"The type of 'genes' you get from your parents has nothing to do with Levi Strauss," she continued. "Instead, they're tiny little chemical messages that are transmitted from parent to child, and they determine such things as the child's facial features, eye color, and height."

Then, she explained that sometimes certain genes only pop up from time to time, so that if you have a father with big feet, you can still have little feet, but you might pass the "big feet" gene on to your kids.

That afternoon, I called my grandparents just as soon as I got home from school. My grandfather answered the phone. Grandma Woo-Woo was at her Garden Club.

"Hi, Granddad," I began, trying to sound as calm as I could.

"Hi, yourself," he replied, happy to hear from me. "How's the world's most beautiful granddaughter?"

My grandfather calls everything about me beautiful. I can't decide whether he really believes it or his eyes are just bad. Either way, I still like it.

"Well," I began slowly. "I was sort of wondering if you have any old family picture albums hanging around your house that I could look at. We were studying about genes and stuff today, and I thought I'd like to take a look at some of my ancestors."

I guess something in my voice told him that it was important. My granddad and I are pretty "in tune."

"Be right over," he said, hardly even taking time to say good-bye.

Twenty minutes later, he was in my living room

with a box of old family albums. On the very front page of my grandfather's album was a picture of my great-grandparents sitting in their yard with all their kids lined up around them.

"Who's that kid standing on the box behind everyone else?" I asked curiously.

Granddad started laughing. "That's my brother, Edward," he chuckled. "But he's not standing on a box. He was just a lot taller than the rest of us. It's a shame you never got to meet Edward. That's probably where you got your beautiful height."

I couldn't believe how relieved I felt. I reached over and hugged my grandfather so tight, I almost choked him. I know it sounds stupid, but knowing where my legs came from gave me a warm feeling of "belonging."

My mother keeps telling me not to worry about my height. She says I just hit my growth spurt early, and now that I'm a teenager, everyone else will start to catch up.

Well, I hate to tell her, but I think she's wrong. I'll turn thirteen officially on October tenth—which just happens to be tomorrow—and so far there's not one kid in my class who can look me in the eye.

2

Happy Birthday to Me

Birthdays are pretty big events at our house. As soon as I get up, my father always snaps my picture. It doesn't matter if my face is all puffy or I'm in my pajamas. Before I get breakfast, I get a flashbulb in the eye. This year I got three. Dad said that since thirteen is a big turning point in a kid's life, he wanted to do things in a big way. I guess you could say he's the sentimental type.

My parents gave me my first big birthday party when I turned one. I can't really remember too much about it, but my father took a picture of me with my ice-cream bowl on my head, so it looks like I was having a pretty good time.

I don't know why, but when I was a baby, my parents took about a thousand pictures of me a week. And for some reason, they especially liked to catch me making some sort of a mess. Besides the picture of the ice-cream bowl on my head, they also have pictures of me playing in the toilet, sitting in a number of different mud puddles, and squeezing tooth paste on my feet. Then, on the piano, they have a large framed picture of me the day that Darrel Kellogg poured lawn mower oil on my head. My mother says the expression on my face is "priceless."

I've found that once kids start growing up and looking like normal people, most of the picture-taking stops. At least that's the way it was with me. Ninety percent of my pictures were taken before I was two. After that, I started looking more like myself. Now, except for birthdays, the only time my parents take a picture of me is when we're on vacation and they need someone to pose in front of a famous rock or something.

After he finished taking my picture, my father hurried out to buy crepe paper and balloons for my party.

"Wait, Dad," I shouted after him. "You don't have to bother with all that. I'm only having two guests."

"It's no bother," he called back. "Besides, maybe if the house looks real festive, more kids will want to come."

"But I don't want more!" I yelled. He didn't hear me, though. He was already on his way to the store. I didn't even have a chance to beg him not to buy hats and horns.

I stopped having big birthday parties in fifth grade. I wanted to stop in the third, but my father seemed so disappointed, I had a couple more just to make him happy. I've always loved going to other kids' big birthday parties, but when it came to my own, I never had a very good time. I know it sounds selfish, but I've always hated watching everyone play with all my new presents.

I think it all started the time Rebecca Wallace pulled the arm off my brand new Barbie doll trying to squeeze her into her new teeny tiny bikini. Rebecca never admitted it, of course. But when I found Barbie sitting in the corner with her arm in her lap, Rebecca was the only one who laughed.

After that, I learned my lesson and started opening my presents right before everyone had to go home. That way, I didn't have to go around saying "Put it down" half the afternoon.

Now that I'm older, I usually invite someone to go to the movies and spend the night. This year, though, since it was a big turning point in my life, I decided to do something different and invite my two best friends, Drew Clayton and Belinda Fischer, to a skating party.

I knew they'd both be excited about it. Drew's the brainy type, so anytime she gets a chance to do something athletic, she considers it a real challenge. Belinda's not brainy, but her mother bought her a red satin skating skirt last Christmas and she likes to wear it every chance she gets. Belinda wants to be a fashion model someday. She says it doesn't matter that she's short and has freckles. She's planning to wear high heels and a lot of make-up.

I realize that going roller skating doesn't sound like a big deal, but I was looking forward to it more than any other birthday I can remember. I guess it was because I knew that I was officially a "teenager."

I know it sounds dumb, but for some reason, I just always thought that when I turned thirteen, something about me would look "different." I don't mean I thought I'd wake up looking like a woman or anything, but "teenagers" just look a lot different than regular twelve-year-olds. So I was sure that when my age finally changed, my looks would just naturally change, too.

I wasn't the only one who thought that, either. When my dad picked my friends up to go to the skating rink that day, Belinda looked a little disappointed.

"You still look the same," she said sadly. I really felt I had let her down.

"I know," I replied. "I have a feeling that looking like a teenager is going to take a little more time than I thought it would. I figure I'll probably start changing sometime in the next few months."

Drew put her hand behind my shoulders. "Did your mom buy you a bra yet?" she asked, feeling for straps.

"Shhh!" I said, embarrassed. "I told you before . . . not in front of . . ." I pointed to the back of my father's head. He probably knows a lot more about women's underwear than I think, but I still feel funny discussing it in front of him.

Even though I was the oldest, I was still the only one who didn't have a bra. Drew needs one. I'm not sure she's really very developed, but she's always been a little on the chubby side, so she can easily fill hers out with baby fat. Belinda sure can't, though. She's even skinnier than I am. She only bought one so that people could see the strap lines through the back of her blouse.

Once we got to the rink and I rented my skates, I realized I wasn't going to have as much fun as I had thought. The roller skates made me look so tall I had to slouch way over so I wouldn't look like a freak. And even slouching, I was still the tallest kid on the floor. One mean boy skated by laughing and shouted, "Hey, Green Giant, what's new in the valley?" Then, every time he and his jerky friend passed us, they would shout "Ho ho ho" in my ear as they whizzed by. I guess after all these years I should be used to "Jolly Green Giant" jokes by now. But I'm not.

"Don't pay any attention to them, Lilli," said Drew. "They're probably just jealous because they're such little runts." I rolled my eyes. Someday, Drew's going to make someone a great mother.

"I think I'll stop for a while and get a soda," I announced suddenly. And before they could say anything, I hurried off the wooden floor of the skating rink and clopped over to the snack bar. Quickly, I plopped down into the first empty chair I saw. Sitting down is always a big relief. It's the only time I feel like I'm a normal size. Conveniently, my chair was right next to the drink machine.

A few minutes later, Drew and Belinda joined me. Drew collapsed in the chair next to me. She's a little out of shape, and I think the weight of the skates was getting to her. Belinda didn't sit. Instead, she kept circling the table, trying to make sure everyone in the snack bar saw her red satin skating skirt. When she was satisfied, she rolled over to the hotdog counter to place an order.

"Be back in a minute," she said. "Ta ta."

Drew looked a little annoyed. "If you ask me," she grumbled, "she looks like one of Santa's helpers." Then, she smoothed out her own baggy corduroy pants and stood up to get a soda.

I continued to eat until I ran out of snack money at two thirty. I know it was two thirty because the man at the microphone said, *"Okay, all you swinging skaters out there . . . it's two thirty and time for another 'couples only' record. So grab your favorite guy or gal and boogie on out to the middle of the floor and get down!"*

I shook my head. "Why is it that whenever someone gets behind a microphone, he always tries to act cool? I bet you a hundred dollars the only time that guy ever says 'boogie' and 'get down' is when he's on the loudspeaker."

Belinda laughed and hurried out of her seat. "Who cares?" she said. "Let's go grab somebody cute and skate!" Belinda is what you'd call the aggressive type.

Reluctantly, Drew stood up and joined her. "I'll

go. But I'm not grabbing," she replied. "Grabbing is demeaning."

"I'll be there in a minute," I assured them. "I need to fix one of my skates."

As I watched the two of them roll away I turned my attention to the front door. Unless King Kong came strolling through, I knew that no boy in the entire place would be tall enough to skate with me.

"Oh, what's the use," I mumbled to myself. And quickly, I reached down, untied both my skates, and pulled them off.

Taking off my skates turned out to be the high point of my day. I'll never forget how good I felt as I stepped down off the rollers to the floor below. It was as if I had suddenly shrunk four inches. For the first time since second grade, I was actually able to look my friends in the eye!

Drew and Belinda kept begging me to skate with them, but I told them my ankles were too weak. I think they believed me. Anytime you're tall and skinny, people think you've got weak ankles. Giraffes have the same problem.

At five o'clock, the rink closed, and when everyone else took their skates off, I went back to being a beanpole again. I called my dad to come get us. He arrived wearing a birthday hat and tooting a horn. I think he was trying to be funny, but sometimes we just don't have the same sense of humor.

When we got home, he passed out hats and horns to everyone. Drew rolled her eyes. "How festive," she mumbled. Belinda chose a red horn to match her skirt.

Mom ushered the three of us into the dining room, where a big birthday cake was waiting, surrounded by presents. Drew begged me to open hers first. It was a new comb and brush set.

"It's made of pure natural boar bristles," she announced proudly.

Belinda wrinkled her nose. "From a dead pig?" she asked squeamishly.

Drew ignored her. "I read somewhere that natural bristles aren't supposed to give you split ends when you brush," she explained.

"Is it from their whiskers or what?" continued Belinda, looking disgusted.

Drew gave her a dirty look and told her, "Look it up."

The next gift I received was from Belinda. Her mother had forgotten about my birthday, so she told Belinda to make some sort of card and stick five dollars in it. Belinda said she wasn't a very good card-maker, so she just pulled the money out of her pocket and handed it to me. I pretended it didn't matter, but the way she did it made me feel like she was paying me for inviting her to my party.

My mom and dad bought me a new stereo. I was really surprised. Usually, they don't buy me a real expensive gift for my birthday. They always say it's too close to Christmas. I think this is a very common excuse for parents to use. Drew says that hers do the same thing, and her birthday's in March.

As usual, the worst present of the day was from Aunt Millie. I can't say that in front of my mother, of course. Whenever my mother hears me being "ungrateful," she always gives me the same speech. "It doesn't matter whether you like the gift or not," she'll say. "It's knowing that someone was kind enough to think of you that counts." Well, I hate to tell her, but I wouldn't care if Aunt Millie never remembered me another day in her life.

Aunt Millie is Grandma Woo-Woo's sister. When I was about three, she flew out to California to see us. I think she was planning to move out here or something. She decided not to move, but for some reason she really took a liking to me. She still lives hundreds of miles away, but every Christmas and birthday Aunt Millie still sends me a gift. The trouble is, I think her memory's gone on the blink, and she can't seem to remember how many years have passed since she's seen me. No matter how old I get, she still sends me stuff for a three-year-old. Last Christmas, for example, she sent me a set of rubber bath toys.

This year, Aunt Millie really outdid herself. She sent me a Little Miss Trudy Beauty Kit. It contained pretend lipstick, fake nail polish, and a dumb little compact with plastic cheek blusher in the center.

As soon as I opened it, Drew and Belinda fell on the floor laughing. I could tell by my mother's expression that she was annoyed with them, but she didn't ruin my birthday by yelling. Instead, she snatched up my Little Miss Trudy gift box and hurried into the kitchen.

A few minutes later, she came out and lit the candles on my cake. Drew and Belinda were still laughing so hard they could hardly sing "Happy Birthday." But once they finally calmed down, everything was quiet while I got ready to make my wishes and blow out the candles.

I realize that thirteen is probably a little old for believing that wishes can come true. Still, no matter how you look at it, it can't hurt. Besides, this year I decided to make my wishes a little more reasonable so that I would have a better chance of having them granted. For three years in a row, I had wished for all the money in the world, and that I would shrink. It was no wonder that I hadn't had much success.

"Hurry up!" urged my mother. "Make your wish and blow. The wax is starting to drip down onto the cake."

I closed my eyes. I've never been too sure who you're supposed to wish to in these situations. I used to think it was your fairy godmother, but that's before I found out she wasn't real. Now I just send up my wishes and hope that they float to the right place.

I squeezed my eyes tightly. Please grant me these three wishes this year, I begged silently. And please keep in mind that I've kept them reasonable. . . . I'd like a bra. I'd like to dance with a boy. And last, but not least, I'd really love to make the Pom Squad for next year.

Then, I opened my eyes and blew with all my might. All the candles went out but one. . . .

3

I Wish I May,
I Wish I Might...

The next day, Drew and I walked home from school together. We only live four houses from each other, so it makes our friendship very convenient.

Drew moved into the neighborhood five years ago when her father was transferred to California from Chicago. I'm not sure what Mr. Clayton does, but I think he's a scientist or some other kind of genius. I'm pretty sure that's where Drew got her brains.

When she first moved in, I didn't like her very much. Even in the third grade, Drew used words with more than eight letters. I remember the first time I met her, she told me that moving had been a very "harrowing" experience for her. I went home and told my mother she was a weirdo.

After I got to know her better, I realized that words like *harrowing* are just a natural part of the way Drew talks. I think her brain is so smart it sends big words out of her mouth before she even has a chance to think about them. The good thing about Drew is that she doesn't look smart. She's sort of pudgy with short brown curly hair. I don't know why, but before I met her I thought all smart people wore Sunday School clothes and glasses.

Sometimes, it's kind of neat to have a "brain" for a friend. No matter what I'm talking about, Drew always seems to have some interesting ideas on the subject, even if I don't always agree with them.

"I made three wishes last night, and all of the candles went out except one," I told her as we headed up our street.

"So what?" she asked, waiting to hear what I was getting at.

"So nothing," I replied, casually shrugging my shoulders. "It's just that I keep wondering if it means that all my wishes will come true but one. Wouldn't that be weird?"

Drew gave me a real disgusted look. "You don't really believe all that birthday-wish garbage, do you, Lilli?" she asked.

Drew doesn't go in for a lot of fantasy stuff. She's the kind of kid who stopped believing in Santa Claus as soon as she saw him in three different stores on the same day. She never fell for the old "helper" story like the rest of us. I think it's probably because she's so intelligent. It might have ruined her imagination.

"Well, do you?" she prodded.

"Of course I don't believe in birthday wishes," I lied. "But you have to admit, it would be weird if only two of them came true."

"That depends on what you wished for," she replied, getting a funny look on her face. "Tell me what your wishes were and I'll see."

"Don't be silly," I said without thinking. "If I told you my wishes, then *none* of them would come true." As soon as I said that, I wanted to take it back. But it was too late.

"Aha!" Drew scoffed. "You fell into my trap! You *do* believe in birthday wishes after all! The next thing you know, you'll be telling me you still believe in Tinkerbell!"

"Don't be ridiculous," I replied smugly. "I happen to know for a fact that Tinkerbell went down in a plane crash near Mexico City six years ago. David Garbanzo told me. It's too bad you never knew David. You two would have a lot in common."

Drew ignored me. "It's not your fault you're an idiot," she said after a second. "It's your parents. I'll never understand why parents spend half their time teaching children not to lie, and they spend the other half lying to them. Imagine teaching kids to believe there's actually a big bunny who lays chocolate eggs!"

"For heaven's sake, Drew," I corrected. "No one said he actually *lays* them. He just delivers them, that's all."

Drew rolled her eyes. "Oh, that's a lot better. A big bunny mail carrier . . . that makes a lot more sense."

"Boy, I'd hate to be a kid of yours," I snapped. "What fun: 'Here, kid. Here's some chocolate eggs. They're made in a factory by a bunch of sweaty men and machines. Happy Easter.' "

"I don't care," said Drew. "It's still better than lying."

"Well, you're wrong about wishes," I argued. "Because for your information, wishes really *can* come true. All you have to do is work, and you can make them happen. Didn't you wish that you would win the state spelling bee last year? And didn't you win it?"

"I studied for it!"

"You wished and you worked and it came true,"

I retorted. "And for your information, Drew Clayton, if an old sourpuss like you can make wishes come true, so can I."

By then, we had arrived at Drew's front porch. She stopped to talk some more, but I just kept walking. I didn't even say good-bye.

I'm sure Drew was surprised. She thinks arguing is a healthy way to exercise the mind. She almost never gets angry like I do. I couldn't help it, though. I know that everyone's entitled to have an opinion, but I don't care how smart you are, you still don't have the right to spoil other people's dreams.

I was two houses down when I heard, "Hey, Lilli! What's up?"

I jumped and turned around. It was Belinda.

"Where'd you come from?" I snapped, still feeling irritated at Drew. "You shouldn't sneak up on people like that."

"I'm sorry," said Belinda apologetically, "but I just can't seem to help it. I guess models are just naturally light on their feet."

I looked down at Belinda's shoes. "Also, it doesn't hurt that you have on rubber soles," I replied.

Belinda was dressed in her soccer uniform. The uniform is the only reason she plays. Our school has the cutest soccer outfits I've ever seen . . . navy-blue shorts and a blue and white sailor shirt. Belinda added a matching headband and wore little anchor barrettes in each side of her hair.

"I can't help the shoes," she explained. "We just had a game after school."

"You win?" I asked, sounding uninterested.

Belinda shrugged. "I don't know. Mr. Wilkerson made me leave before it started. He got mad because I was trying to make French braids in my hair during warm-up exercises. I'm thinking about quitting. Want to go home and try on my uniform? Maybe you could fill in as my replacement."

"No, thanks," I grumbled. "I don't look good in sailor suits."

I didn't mention it to Belinda, but soccer isn't really one of my best sports. When I was in the third grade, my parents signed me up for a girls' soccer team to help improve my coordination. Some help. During the first game, Julie Giles tried passing me the ball, but my legs got going so fast they went out of control. Not only did I outrun the ball, but when I got to the end of the field, I tripped and rolled into the goal. My arm got caught under the net, and my coach had to stop the game to get me out. I thought I would die.

"You in a bad mood or something?" asked Belinda, studying my face.

"Oh, it's that stupid Drew," I blurted. "Sometimes she just makes me so mad. She just got finished telling me how dumb it was for me to make birthday wishes."

Belinda nodded understandingly. "That sounds like something she'd say. Just don't pay any attention to her. If wishes couldn't come true, then why would we all have fairy godmothers to grant them?"

I stared at her for a minute, but I didn't say anything. It's really amazing how I can have such different friends.

"Maybe Drew's right," I said at last. "Maybe it's time I grew up and faced reality. Maybe making wishes really *is* just fantasy and pretend."

Belinda wrinkled her forehead as if she was doing some serious thinking. "You might be right," she replied finally. "But as long as it doesn't hurt anybody, I think I'd just go on pretending it's real."

I thought about what she said and then began to smile. Belinda may not be as bright as Drew, but sometimes she makes a lot more sense.

4

Wish Number One

The more I thought about what Drew had said, the more determined I became about making my wishes come true. And even though she didn't know it, Drew was the main reason I succeeded in wish number one.

I know that to a lot of girls getting their first bra isn't a big deal at all. I've even heard of girls who actually have to be *forced* by their mothers to wear one. But to me, not wearing a bra was just another thing that made me "different." And in my opinion, being five six is enough of a difference for anyone.

It wasn't so bad at first. In September, a lot of the seventh graders didn't wear them. But one by one, more and more bras kept showing up, until by the middle of October, almost every girl in my gym class was wearing one.

I hated it. Gym class was bad enough without having to huddle in the corner and try to secretly wriggle out of your clothes while everyone else paraded around in adult underwear. Also, it didn't help matters any that my locker was right next to Queenie Paxton's.

Queenie Paxton is the kind of girl whose hobby is making fun of others. She moved to our school in September and always talks with this real faky southern accent. One time, Drew asked her what part of the South she was from and Queenie said South Dakota. She's not very bright, but for a seventh grader, she's the most "developed" girl I've ever seen. Drew says she's actually a twenty-three-year-old with short legs.

Ever since we first changed clothes in the girls' locker room, Queenie has always made fun of me. "There's no sense tryin' to keep yourself covered, Lillian honey," she'd say in her phoniest southern accent. "Everyone already knows you're flat as a pancake." Or "Hey, Lilli! Made any mountains out of your lil' ole molehills yet?"

The rest of the girls were real nice about it. They were always telling her to shut up and stuff. Drew told me not to pay any attention to her. "Everyone knows Queenie's a jerk, Lilli," she would say. "No one even listens to a word she says."

No one except me, I thought. I tried not to, but Queenie made me feel so bad, once I went to the nurse's office just so I wouldn't have to go to gym.

The week after my birthday, Queenie really outdid herself. She came waltzing into the locker room and stood in front of me grinning from ear to ear. "Hey, Green Giant," she said, pretending to shout up to me. "How are your niblets growing?"

I felt the tears begin to flood my eyes. But before she could see my tears, Drew stepped in.

"Hey, Paxton," she said angrily. "Why don't you pick on someone your own size . . . like a maggot, for instance?"

After that, Queenie left me alone. But the rest of the day, I couldn't get her mean grin out of my mind. And what made it even worse was that in sixth period, I sat behind Belinda. And since Belinda is smaller than most fourth graders and truly does not need a bra at all, sitting there staring at her straps through the back of her blouse made me doubly depressed.

Drew sensed how upset I was and after school showed up at my bedroom door ready to talk. I knew she would. Last year, Drew did a report on psychiatrists, and ever since then she tries to force everyone to talk about their problems. Drew says that facing your problems is the first step to complete mental health.

"Listen, Lillian," she began, not even waiting for me to invite her in. "I've been doing a lot of thinking about this Queenie Paxton thing, and I've decided it's time for you to ask your mother for a bra."

I stared at her for a second, and then covered my head with my pillow. I'm not always as willing to talk as Drew would like. Quickly, she walked over and uncovered my head.

"As I was saying, even though sometimes it's very important to be an individual and not follow the crowd, once in a while it's just as important to join in. And it's my opinion that the time is ripe for you to get a bra."

"Ripe?" I asked, embarrassed, trying to get the pillow back. She was making me sound like a cantaloupe.

Drew sat down on the edge of my bed. Her voice got much softer. "You know what I mean, Lillian. I just can't stand to see Queenie hurt you anymore. Why don't you ask your mother to buy you one?"

"I can't!" I blurted, nervous at the thought of it. "I just can't. She wouldn't do it. I think she's waiting until I . . . well, you know . . . really *need* one."

"How do you know?" asked Drew. "You've never even tried. I bet you anything if you explained the situation, she'd want what's best for you."

I rolled my eyes. "That's the trouble. What I think is best and what my mother thinks is best are usually two different things. Have you forgotten that we're talking about the same woman who insisted on signing me up for cello lessons two years ago?"

Drew started laughing, but it wasn't funny. Not to me, at least. Lugging that stupid cello back and forth to school had been one of the worst experiences of my life, and I wasn't completely over it yet. All I had done was raise my hand when Miss Blossom, our music teacher, had asked the class, "How many of you would like to be as rich and famous as Beethoven was?" If you raised your hand, you got a note sent home saying, "Your child has expressed an interest in playing a string instrument."

I tried to explain the whole thing to my mother, but she wouldn't listen. She was so excited about the note that she got right on the phone and signed me up for lessons that same afternoon. My mother plays the piano, and I think she had visions of the two of us going on the road as an opening act for Willie Nelson or something.

Her excitement didn't last long, though. I only

took cello lessons for three months before she and my father begged me to stop. They said that the noises coming from the living room at night when I practiced were making it hard for them to digest their dinner. My mother suggested that I practice in the morning, but my father said that breakfast was the most important meal of the day, and he just couldn't risk it. That's when I quit.

"Never mind about the stupid cello," said Drew, still chuckling to herself. "This is different. Believe me, Lillian, if there is one thing a mother really can't stand, it's to have her daughter laughed at and ridiculed by others. Trust me on this. I read it in *Parents* magazine."

"Really?" I asked finally. "You really read something like that?"

"Sort of. Now what do you say? Are you going to get the nerve to ask her tonight, or are you going to subject yourself to another showdown with Queenie Paxton? The choice is yours."

"Some wonderful choice," I mumbled. But deep inside, I knew what my answer had to be.

That night after dinner, I waited for my father to leave the table. Then, I started to help my mother with the dishes. I could tell she was surprised, because usually I don't help with stuff unless I get yelled at.

"Gee, what a good girl," she said, reaching over to give me a quick hug. Whenever I do something nice, she hugs me. I think it's supposed to encourage me to do it again.

After the table was cleared, I felt myself begin to get very nervous. It's really funny. Usually, I'm not afraid to talk to my mother at all. But lately, when it comes to real personal stuff, I get sweaty palms. That's the reason I like to wait until she's busy in the kitchen. Discussing bras while someone is scraping plates is a lot easier than sitting down and looking them in the eye. Still, it wasn't simple. I guess that's why I waited until she turned on the garbage disposal before I popped the question.

". . . so I thought I'd sort of like one, too," I concluded after the disposal was turned off.

"Like one what?" asked my mother. "Honestly, Lillian, why do you always have so much to say when the garbage disposal's on?" Then she laughed and began to wipe the counter.

I dried my sweaty hands on the dish towel and took a deep breath. "Well . . . uh . . . I was just saying that practically all the other girls in my class are wearing . . . you know . . . bras now. And I was just thinking that maybe I should have one, too. Even Belinda Fischer has one."

My mother stopped what she was doing and

looked up, surprised. After a second, she started to chuckle. "Belinda Fischer has a bra?" she giggled. "You're kidding? She doesn't need one any more than you do."

Feeling uncomfortable, I forced a small "heh-heh" and a weak smile.

"I just don't understand it, honey," continued my mother. "Why is everyone always in such a hurry to grow up? Belinda hasn't even started to develop *up there* yet."

When she said "up there," I wanted to die.

"You're going to be an adult all your life, Lillian," added Mom as she walked over and tousled my hair. "Take some time to be young while you can. Besides," she said smiling, "you don't want to be exactly like everyone else, do you? Be an individual. Don't be afraid to be different. After all, if all your friends jumped in the lake, would you jump in the lake, too?"

I didn't tell her, but I might. It would just depend on how much I wanted to get out of the heat. My heart began to pound faster and faster. I wished I didn't have to talk about it anymore. But I did. I couldn't face Drew tomorrow if I didn't see it through.

"It's not just because of Belinda that I want one," I continued slowly. "There's also this girl named Queenie Paxton. . . ."

"Queenie?" chuckled my mother. "What kind of a name is Queenie?"

"She's awful, Mom. You should hear the things she says to me when we change for gym class. I'm practically the only one in there without a bra, and she keeps comparing me to molehills and pancakes and . . ."

I had to stop. When I heard myself say pancakes, my eyes started to fill with tears. I swallowed hard and continued.

". . . and niblets!" I blurted at last. "Oh, God, Mother . . . niblets, of all things. . . ."

The tears spilled over onto my cheeks. Mom got me a tissue and dabbed them away. "I'd almost forgotten how cruel kids can be," she whispered.

"Don't you see, Mom?" I sobbed. "Sometimes, it's just too hard to be different. I'm not trying to grow up too fast. All I want to do is fit in a little better."

My mother put her arms around me and sighed. "I know that sometimes life is very hard, honey. But you can't always let people like Queenie Paxton run your life for you. Sometimes, you have to stand your ground against people like that and fight for the right to be yourself."

I couldn't believe what I was hearing. "For heaven's sake, Mother!" I yelled. "This isn't the Civil

War! Why can't you just understand? I *am* myself! All I want you to do is make being me a little easier!"

Then, before she could reach out and hug me again, I ran out of the kitchen as fast as I could. When I got to my room, I locked the door behind me. I thought I heard my mother calling for me to come back, but I didn't go.

Later, I heard her go out somewhere in the car, so I took the opportunity to take a quick bath and get in bed. I had already decided I would go to the nurse again during gym class the next day.

The next morning when I woke up, I was surprised to find a white plastic bag from Bradford's department store at the end of my bed. Attached to the outside was a note from my mother.

Dear Lillian,
      I'm not trying to make your life harder, honey. I'm really not. I love you.
                                    Mom

Inside, wrapped in tissue paper, were three bras.

5

Penguins, Anyone?

At school, Drew and Belinda were the very first ones to congratulate me on the new "strap marks" showing through the back of my blouse. Well, actually, they were the *only* ones. I guess most people don't think getting a bra deserves congratulations. I mean, Hallmark doesn't make a card for it or anything.

Drew patted me on the back. "I knew your mother would come through. What'd I tell you? *Parents* magazine is never wrong."

It was all I could do to keep from telling her it was a "wish come true." I didn't, though. I guess I'll always feel that birthday wishes are just too personal to blab about. Besides, now that the first wish had come true, all I wanted to do was begin to concentrate on the second one . . . dancing with a boy.

Dancing with a boy was something I had dreamed about for years . . . ever since I got Billy Bartholemew for a square dance partner in the second grade. As a dancer, Billy really stunk. But I couldn't help thinking that with a few quick lessons at the Arthur Murray Dance Studio, the two of us would have made a wonderful couple. Unfortunately, by third grade, even though Billy had his feet under better control, I was at least three inches taller than any boy in the class, so my dancing dreams went right down the toilet. And that's where they had stayed until the evening I blew out the candles on my thirteenth birthday cake.

Finally, after all those years, I had decided to stop being so stubborn. If I wanted to dance, it would simply have to be with someone shorter, and that was that. Once I had made up my mind, I could hardly wait for the next big dance to make it come true.

At Butterfield Junior High, the Christmas Dance is the biggest event of the year. Even when I was still in elementary school, I remember Drew's older sister, Melanie, talking about how neat it was. Melanie said that the decorations made her feel like she was in a "winter wonderland of ice and snow."

44

The Christmas Dance is sponsored by the seventh grade. The eighth grade sponsors the Spring Fling, but according to Melanie, it's not nearly as popular. As soon as school started this year, I decided that I wanted to be on the Christmas Dance Decoration Committee since I'm really a pretty good artist. I think I get it from my granddad. He was a house painter. A lot of people don't think that house painters are really artistic, but if they could see my grandfather blend colors and paint trim, they'd change their minds.

The idea that a bunch of kids could transform a dirty old gym into a "winter wonderland of ice and snow" really fascinated me. I had even spent time imagining how I would go about decorating if I was in charge. It would be almost like being a magician.

Finally, the first week of November, a sign-up sheet was posted in the hall. And I was very lucky, as it turned out, because I was standing right next to the bulletin board when the school secretary tacked it up. Immediately, I took out a pencil and printed my name in the first line under *Decoration Committee.*

I figured it would fill up pretty fast, and I was right. Belinda signed up right after I did. But later that day, when Drew tried, it was all filled in, and she had to take the refreshment committee instead.

In a way, I was kind of glad. Drew's not very artistic, and I was afraid she might mess things up. When we were little, she ruined my favorite coloring book by giving Snow White purple hair. I've never really forgiven her for that.

The first meeting of the decoration committee was held November sixth. I was glad it was going to be in my homeroom. Being in familiar surroundings always helps put me at ease. Unfortunately, by the time I got there, icky Harold Dunbar had already plopped down in my seat. I tried explaining that it was mine, but Harold said that just because I sat there for ten minutes in the morning didn't mean I owned it. That really made me furious. I'm very possessive about my seat, and knowing that Harold Dunbar's germs were running all over the top of my desk really annoyed me, especially when he started cleaning his fingernails.

Irritated, I took a seat as far away from Harold as I could get. Belinda slid into the seat next to me. "Gosh," she said, looking around. "This place is really filling up. I bet Drew could show up for this committee and no one would know the difference. Maybe I should go try to find her."

I rolled my eyes. "Go right ahead," I snapped, still angry at Harold. "But don't be surprised when the gym is filled with a bunch of purple-haired Santas."

Belinda gave me a funny look, but before she could say anything, Mrs. Knutson walked through the door. Mrs. Knutson was the teacher in charge of organizing the decorations. Everyone knew she had come into the room, but no one got quiet. After three o'clock, teachers don't seem quite as threatening.

After looking around the room a minute, Mrs. Knutson walked over to her desk and waited for things to settle down. But, if anything, the talking just got louder. Finally, she gave up waiting and started glaring. Mrs. Knutson is the best glarer I have ever seen. I have her for Social Studies, so I'm pretty familiar with the way she does it. First, she makes her eyes real squinty; then she pulls her lips so tight they almost disappear.

Once she started glaring, things quieted down real fast. "That's better," she said at last. "Now then, before we can get started on the decorations, the first thing we have to do is decide upon a theme for the dance. Are there any suggestions?"

Suddenly, everyone began screaming at once, trying to get Mrs. Knutson's attention. I think most of them were asking what a theme was, but the noise got so loud, you couldn't hear yourself think. Finally, I had to cover my ears.

Personally, I'm not much of a screamer. It's not that there's anything wrong with my voice. It's just that I don't like to call a lot of attention to myself. I usually get enough just by standing up. Besides, this time I was so busy giving Harold Dunbar the evil eye, I didn't have a chance.

After a few seconds, I heard a sharp crack in the front of the room and looked up. Mrs. Knutson was standing there slamming a wooden ruler on her desk top. Everyone shut up immediately. A teacher slamming a wooden ruler is an internationally known symbol for silence.

"Lillian Pinkerton," said Mrs. Knutson, looking at me. "Since you were the only one in the room polite enough not to scream, I'd like to hear any ideas you might have as to what the theme of the dance should be. Have you given it any thought, dear?"

I hate it when a teacher calls me dear. I know they mean well, but it makes me feel like their pet or something. And frankly, I've got enough problems without adding that one.

One by one, everyone in the room turned around and began staring at me. I felt my face getting red and my mouth went dry.

Finally, I took a deep breath, cleared my throat, and nodded. "Penguins," I said quietly.

I hardly had the word out of my mouth before everyone began to laugh. In the back of the room, Danny Dabovitch fell out of his chair. Mrs. Knutson picked up her ruler again, but laughing is a lot harder to control than screaming, and it took several slams for things to settle back down.

"I think we all owe Lillian an apology," she said at last. "And from now on, I expect you to have the common courtesy to listen to an idea before you reject it. Now then, Lillian dear, exactly what do you mean by penguins?"

Once again, all eyes were back on me and my red face.

"Well . . . I just thought that since every year at Christmas most of the attention is given to the North Pole, it might be sort of nice if we did something on the South Pole for a change. We could have cardboard icebergs, snowflakes, icicles, and lots of little penguins all over the place. One time I read that penguins can only be found at the South Pole, and well . . . I just thought it would be sort of different, that's all."

When I was finished, I looked up. No one was laughing anymore. Instead, a couple of the kids had actually begun to shake their heads in agreement.

Belinda reached over and patted me on the shoulder. "Way to go, Lilli," she said proudly. "I never knew you were that imaginative."

Mrs. Knutson looked pretty proud herself. "There, see?" she said. "If you just give a person a chance to explain, sometimes their ideas don't turn out to be as dumb as they sound."

Mrs. Knutson wrote *Penguins* on the board and then turned back to the class. "Any other suggestions?"

Candy Cooper raised her hand. "I think we ought to make the gym into a big Candyland," she said in her disgustingly sweet little voice. I should have known she'd come up with something like that. Candy thinks that "Candy" is just about the most darling name in the world.

"You know," she continued, "we could have giant candy canes and big candy kisses all over the place. Wouldn't that be cute?"

Behind me, Michael Grubb made a noise like someone was throwing up. I didn't blame him. The idea made me sick, too. But Mrs. Knutson just ignored him and wrote *Candyland* right under *Penguins*.

After that, there were only two more suggestions. Patricia Hoosier wanted her father to dress up as

Santa Claus and sit on a big throne under one of the basketball nets. She said that kids could sit on his lap and have their pictures taken. If you liked the picture, you could give him a tip. I think Mr. Hoosier was out of work or something.

Michael Grubb was the only boy with a suggestion. He wanted to do a "Christmas in Space" theme. He said that we could have people dress up like robots and sit in the corners of the gym. Then, as soon as the dance was over, they could spring up and shoot everyone with laser guns. Mrs. Knutson scowled. She said she wasn't sure what killing people with lasers had to do with Christmas, but she put it down anyway. Social studies teachers are very democratic.

Once all the suggestions were in, it was time to vote. Quickly, I scribbled a note to Belinda begging her to vote for *Penguins*. I knew it wouldn't do any good though. Belinda always waits to see what everyone else is voting for and then joins in. I don't really blame her. There's nothing more embarrassing than shooting your hand in the air to vote for something and then finding out that it's up there waving all alone. Drew says it makes you look like an individual. But I think it just makes you look like you've got bad taste.

This time I didn't have a choice. When Mrs. Knutson called out "Penguins," I swallowed hard, raised my hand slowly, and hoped for the best.

At first it was pretty scary. It looked as if everyone else was still trying to make up their minds. I tried to give Belinda an "up" sign with my other hand, but she wouldn't look at me. Finally, one by one, different kids around the room started raising their hands. I've never been so relieved in my life, and surprised. By the end of the counting, Penguins had received thirteen votes. Belinda was number twelve.

"Okay," said Mrs. Knutson after she finished tallying the score. "How many of you would like Candyland?"

Michael Grubb made the throw-up sound again, and everyone laughed—everyone except Candy, that is. She pretended not to hear, and raised her hand high into the air. After the laughter died down, five of her friends joined her.

Mrs. Knutson moved on to suggestion number three. "Who wants Mr. Hoosier?" she asked bluntly.

I felt kind of sorry for Patricia. Besides her own vote, there was only one other. It was Sally Kelley. Sally's father owns Kelley's Costume Shop, so I'm sure she figured they could make some money by renting Mr. Hoosier his Santa suit.

When Mrs. Knutson got to Michael Grubb's suggestion, she just pointed to it. I guess she just couldn't bring herself to say lasers again. Naturally, all the boys voted for it. But there were only four of them, so I didn't have to worry.

"Well," said Mrs. Knutson, gazing over the voting totals. "It looks like we've got a theme for this year's Christmas dance—penguins. Although maybe Christmas at the South Pole would sound a little nicer. Does that meet with everyone's approval?"

A few heads nodded here and there.

"Good," said Mrs. Knutson. "Now then, Lillian . . . since it was your idea, how would you like to be chairperson of the decoration committee?"

I took a deep breath and smiled nervously. I had never been chairperson of anything before, but I knew I couldn't pass up the chance to try.

"Well . . . okay," I replied quietly as everyone turned around to stare at me some more.

This time, though, their stares didn't bother me as much. Being chairperson made me feel sort of big. And *big* was definitely a nice change from tall.

Drew was elected head of the refreshment committee. I suggested that since we were both chairpersons, maybe we could coordinate the refreshments with the decorations. "Maybe you guys could have Penguin Punch," I offered cleverly. "Or how about Snowflake Cookies?"

Drew looked insulted and told me that if I didn't mind, refreshments were her domain. In other words, butt out.

I could tell my parents were really proud that I had finally been elected the leader of something. They told everyone they knew. Parents really love it when you show leadership. It makes them think they're raising you right.

The decorating committee took a lot more time than I thought it would. The dance was going to be on the fifteenth of December, but there was so much to do I wasn't sure if five weeks would be enough time. I called three meetings after school each week in the art room, but usually only about ten or eleven kids showed up.

The first thing I did was assign each person a project to work on. Since the boys seemed to want to work together, I asked them to construct the icebergs. It was going to be a big project, and I figured it would keep them busy and out of trouble. If you don't keep boys busy, they end up wrestling around or playing "keep away" with the art supplies.

While the boys began gathering material for their icebergs, the rest of us got to work cutting out snowflakes and icicles. I had planned to hang them from the ceiling, and I wanted to have enough snowflakes so it would really look like it was snowing.

The biggest project was the penguins, so I asked everyone to make at least two life-size models. I suggested that they be made of cloth and stuffing or papier-mâché, and since the school didn't have all the extra supplies on hand, they had to be made at home.

Sally Kelley raised her hand. "Speaking of stuffing, I can bring in a giant snowman suit from the shop, and we can stuff it with newspaper."

I didn't want to hurt her feelings, but the last thing I wanted was a giant snowman. Since no one lives at the South Pole, snowmen don't even exist down there. I tried to be as nice about it as I could.

"Well . . . thanks anyway, Sally," I began. "But, ah . . . the thing is . . . they don't actually have people living at the South Pole, so there probably aren't any snowmen, either."

Sally got huffy. "The penguins could have made it!" she snapped. "What do you think they've got those little flippers for?"

Patricia Hoosier came over and whispered something in Sally's ear. Only she didn't exactly "whisper." She said I was acting like a big know-it-all. So just to keep peace, I gave in and told Sally she could bring her stupid snowman if she wanted to.

Candy Cooper wasn't very cooperative, either. Almost every time we had a meeting, I kept catching her in the back of the art room coloring in candy canes. I asked her nicely to stop. But she just turned up her nose and said there was no law against making peppermint sticks.

Luckily, the rest of the kids were a lot easier to get along with than Sally and Candy. By the end of the fourth week, we had hundreds of snowflakes ready for hanging, and the boys were putting the finishing touches on the two enormous icebergs. They really turned out neat. Each was made out of poster board and stood over five feet high. They had covered the top of both icebergs with clear blue cellophane to make them look real icy, and had sprayed the rest with fake snow.

Ronald Galloway offered to bring a few towels from home to spread on the floor around them. "That way," he explained, "it'll make it seem like they're really melting."

Michael Grubb punched him in the arm and said it was the stupidest idea he'd ever heard.

6

Granddad
to the Rescue

I was just as busy at home as I was in school. Since
I was the head of the committee, I wanted to make
sure my penguins were extra special, so I asked my
granddad for help. I would have asked my father,
but he's not really the handyman type. Once he tried
to hang a ceiling fan in the kitchen, and during the
night it fell through the middle of our kitchen table.
My mother said it was a miracle that no one was
killed.

Anyway, the first night Granddad came to work
on the penguins, he showed up with so much wood
and chicken wire it looked like he was going to erect

a building or something. At first it made me very nervous.

"Ah . . . listen, Granddad," I said, trying not to offend him. "I'm not sure that you really understood what I want to do here. See . . . the thing is . . . these penguins only have to be a couple of feet tall."

Granddad nodded and went to get another load of materials from his truck. "Yup. I got'cha," he said on his way out the door.

When he got back, I followed him to the garage with a yardstick. He said there was still another load of stuff in his truck and I was really beginning to panic. I stopped him before he went outside again.

"Look, Granddad," I said, pointing to the twenty-four-inch mark on the yardstick. "This is two feet. See how little it is?"

"Yup," he said again, and off he went.

I slumped down in the corner of the garage and covered my eyes. There was enough material there to build a penguin eight feet tall. "I can see it all now," I mumbled to myself, "The Penguin Who Ate Chicago."

Granddad finished bringing in his equipment and patted me on the head. "Don't worry, honey," he said reassuringly. "Old Gramps has been around long enough to know how big two feet is. Now then, let's get started."

First, Granddad took some wire cutters from his tool box and snipped the chicken wire into smaller pieces. Then he showed me how to bend it into the shape of a penguin's body. He was really a perfectionist. He wasn't satisfied until I brought out an encyclopedia so we could get the shape just right. Then we started on the head and beak.

Altogether, it took four nights of bending and shaping before the penguin frames were finished and we could nail them onto the wooden bases he had made. I was beginning to see why he needed so much material. There were a lot of things we needed that I just hadn't thought about.

Once the frames and bases were all set, the two of us got to work on the papier-mâché to cover them. It was something I was really dreading. I've always hated papier-mâché. It sounds neat, but once you find out it's nothing but old newspaper soaked in flour and water, it's a big disappointment. A better name for it would be paper-glop.

"I've got to be honest with you, Granddad," I said as he was mixing it all together. "I'm not very creative with this stuff. One time in art, we had to use it to make a Creatures of the Forest exhibit, and my creature didn't turn out very well. I tried making a beaver, but his tail kept falling off. It ended up looking like a basketball with buck teeth."

Granddad patted me on the shoulder. "Don't worry. We'll see that that doesn't happen again. The trick to papier-mâché is to apply it to the frame in thin sheets." Then he took a thin piece of torn newspaper, dipped it in the glop, and laid it smoothly on the frame of the penguin.

"That's it?" I asked, amazed. Granddad smiled and offered me the glop. I took the newspaper and did the same thing. When I was finished, mine looked as smooth as his.

For the next few hours, the two of us took turns dipping and smoothing, smoothing and dipping. Carefully, we covered each part of the frames, from beaks to flippers to feet.

When we were finished, I stood back to look at them. "I can't believe it," I said, delighted. "Just look at them. They look exactly like penguins!"

Granddad hurried into the house and brought out a measuring stick. "Two feet on the button!" he said, proudly measuring the first one. The second was a little smaller. He said it probably hadn't eaten enough fish as a baby.

I laughed and hugged him as tightly as I could. "They'll look even better when we get them painted," he said when I finally released my grip on his neck.

He was right, too. Once the papier-mâché had

dried, a few coats of black and white paint made them almost come alive. I let Granddad do most of the painting though. For a while I tried, and did a pretty good job. But when I got to the face, my penguin kept turning out with this ridiculous little red grin.

The more I tried to fix it, the bigger and redder the grin became. When I was finished, it looked like Penguin the Clown.

"I hate it!" I said angrily, almost pushing it down. "It looks ridiculous!"

Granddad looked over at what I had done. "No, it doesn't," he replied, trying to keep a straight face. "It just looks a little . . . well . . . happier than most penguins."

Tears started filling my eyes. I tried wiping them away before Granddad could see, but I think he knew. Quickly, he took my penguin and painted over his wild grin. Then, when he had finished adding a few extra touches to its mouth, he stood the two penguins side by side.

"Well? What d'ya think, little girl?" he said, taking my hand and standing back so we could get a good look.

"They look like they just walked into the garage from the South Pole," I replied. And this time, when we hugged, I didn't stop until my arms ached.

I'll never forget how proud I was when I finally took them to school for the last committee meeting. When I carried them in the art room that morning, I couldn't help noticing how everyone was smiling at them. Not snickering or giggling, but smiling, the same way a cute penguin makes you smile when you see one waddle across your TV screen.

After school, the kids in the decorating committee really loved them. "Wow!" shouted Michael Grubb. "How'd you get them so real-looking? What'd you do, shoot a couple?"

I smiled casually. "Papier-mâché."

Michael set his two penguins next to mine. "I used papier-mâché, too," he admitted, looking a bit disturbed. "But mine didn't come out that good."

I looked at his penguins closely. One of them looked like a bumpy black and white football with a beak. The other one was wearing an evil grin and had a large silver object attached to its left wing.

"It's a laser gun," Michael explained. "I thought it was only fair."

Before I could say anything, Patricia Hoosier came up behind me and tapped me on the back. "Here," she said, shoving two small black cut-outs in my direction. "Want these?"

I took the two small papers in my hand and examined them. "Crows?" I asked curiously.

Patricia gave me a dirty look. "They're not crows," she snapped. "They happen to be penguins."

Michael Grubb started to laugh. "They were supposed to be life-size, you idiot," he said.

"They are life-size!" insisted Patricia. "That's how small they look from the ground when they're flying. You're supposed to hang them from the ceiling."

I sat down slowly at a nearby desk and tried to stay calm. "Patricia," I began, trying to put it as nicely as I could, "penguins don't fly. They walk and swim, and once in a while they slide, but they haven't been able to fly for millions of years. If I suspended them from the ceiling, it would look like they were hanging themselves."

Patricia didn't take the news well. Her face got so red, I thought she was going to explode. Then she snatched her penguins out of my hand and stomped out of the room. "I quit this stupid committee!" she said as she left. "It's stupid, and I hate it!"

Sally Kelley ran after her to try to calm her down. Neither one of them ever came back.

After that, everyone else on the committee started wandering in carrying penguins of various shapes and sizes. I never knew that the term *life-size* could mean so many different things.

Harold Frasier's were the biggest. He looked a

little embarrassed when he set them down. They were bigger than the icebergs. "I thought life-size meant as big as people," he muttered quietly.

Danny Dabovitch hurried in carrying a small stuffed animal under his arm. He told me that his paper route didn't leave him much time for making penguins, so he had "borrowed" one from his sister's bed. Most of its fur was gone, and it was missing an eye. "The dog chewed it up," explained Danny. "But we could just pretend it was the result of a polar bear attack."

Even though all the penguins weren't perfect, by the time we got them all standing together in the back of the room, they really looked cute. Altogether, there were twenty-five of them, and I smiled with pride when I saw what my leadership had accomplished.

After everyone left the art room, I stayed behind for a few minutes and lined up the penguins, two by two, as if they were in a parade. Then, I carefully picked up the two my granddad and I had made and put them in the front.

After I was finished, I gathered my books together and turned out the lights. Then I took one more proud look at my wonderful penguin parade before I closed the door.

7

The Dance

The night of the dance, Drew came over to let me do her hair. When it comes to history, Drew can name almost every battle of the Civil War. But when it comes to fluffing her hair up a little, she's a total moron. I used to think it was because her fingers were too chubby. But now, I just think it's nature's way of equaling things out.

Luckily, hair has never really been a problem for me. I guess it's just another thing I'm good at growing. Even when I was a baby, I never went bald like most kids do. I just sort of went from "fuzzy" to "hair," all in one step. Right now it's light blond, but my mother says it'll probably turn darker. Brown-haired people are always saying stuff like that.

When Drew and I were finally ready, we went downstairs. As soon as we hit the bottom step, my father started smiling. "Va-va-va-voom!" he said loudly. I knew he'd say that. It happens every time I get dressed up to go somewhere. I don't know exactly what va-va-va-voom means, but when I get a little older, I think I'll ask him to knock it off.

I did look nice, though, even for a beanpole. My mother had bought me a new pair of white designer corduroys and a red silk shirt. I think she was a little disappointed that I wasn't getting more dressed up. While we were shopping, she kept trying to interest me in this long, red velvet skirt. I didn't want to hurt her feelings, but it looked like something Mrs. Santa Claus would wear.

Anyway, when she finally saw me in my new clothes, she pulled me aside and told me I looked beautiful. Beautiful enough to dance with? I thought to myself. I hadn't forgotten about my second wish for a minute, and I couldn't think of a more perfect time for it to happen than at the Christmas Dance I had helped to create.

Since Drew and I were both chairing committees, we had to be at the dance thirty minutes early. On the way, we picked up Belinda. I told her I'd use my influence to get her in early. She and Drew laughed. Finally, I did too. But, I hadn't really meant it as a joke.

When we walked into the gym, the decorations looked even more beautiful than they had when we'd finished with them that afternoon. On the far wall were the words WE COME TO THE SOUTH PO E. Drew stood there a minute and scratched her head. "We come to the South Poe?" she said. "What the heck does that mean?"

"It means the two *L*'s fell on the floor," I said, hurrying over to pick them up. Belinda went off to find some tape.

Once the letter was back in place, I took another look around. Everything else looked just perfect. The gym was just light enough to make everything visible and just dark enough to hide the mistakes.

Up above my head, hundreds of snowflakes and icicles dangled in the air. Two large icebergs rose from the far corners of the room. Scurrying around the bottom of each iceberg were lots of little penguins. One wore a sign that said DO NOT TOUCH THE PENGUINS. On his side, he packed a silver laser gun. Michael Grubb's idea. He said it would look like we meant business.

After I finished my inspection, I walked over to the refreshment table. Drew was standing there arranging things.

"Munchies?" she asked, spreading her arms out the length of the table.

I looked over the selection. There were about forty bowls of pretzels and a bowl of green punch. "Who's bringing the rest of the food?" I asked curiously. "Aren't you having cake or cookies or something?"

Drew gave me a dirty look. "We're not catering a wedding here, Lillian," she snapped. "Pretzels and Kool Aid are perfect for a Christmas Dance. Look how festive the red and green colors look next to each other."

I never really thought of pretzels as being red, but I didn't feel like arguing about it.

Just then, Ernest Poinsett dashed behind me with his arms full of records. He was the entire music committee, and had volunteered to work the stereo all night.

I noticed that the front of his shirt was unbuttoned, and he was wearing about six gold chains. I think he was taking his deejay job a little too seriously.

Ernest Poinsett is one of those spooky kids that no one knows much about. I've gone to school with him for seven years now, and he still turns his head the other way when we pass each other in the hall. I used to think he was just shy. But last year, for the talent show, he played the French horn and sang, "I Left My Heart in San Francisco," in front of a million people. So now, I don't know what to think.

By the time Ernest got the stereo working and the first record on, kids had already started coming through the door. A few had even started dancing. Belinda and I stood near Drew at the refreshment table for a while. We did a few steps to the music, but it wasn't like we were dancing with each other or anything.

My mother says that when she was my age, girls used to fast dance with each other all the time. She told me that she and her sister used to practice new steps at home and then show off at all the dances. Sometimes, I wish she wouldn't tell me stuff like that. The thought of my mother swinging Aunt Betty around the dance floor disturbs me.

Belinda waited for the start of the third record. It was a slow one, and as soon as she heard it, she took off to find someone to dance with. Belinda has more guts than anyone else I know. If she feels like dancing, she just goes right over to a boy and asks him. She doesn't even have to stand around working up her nerve.

Drew's a little different. When it comes to boys, she's not quite as bold as Belinda. But if anyone does ask her, she's on the dance floor quick as a flash. Drew will dance with anybody. It doesn't matter how disgusting he is. Drew says that just because a person is a scumball, it doesn't mean he's a bad dancer.

While we were standing there, Ernest Poinsett ran up behind her and grabbed for her hand. "Come on," he said. "Quick. I don't have much time between records."

Trying to look cool, Ernest had unbuttoned his shirt even further. He didn't look cool, though; mostly, he just looked undressed. Drew raced after him onto the dance floor.

I stood there for a minute alone and smiled at anyone who passed. Smiling is very important when you're standing alone. It keeps you from looking so pitiful. Another trick I use when I'm standing alone, is to wipe my forehead a lot. That way it looks like I've been dancing, got overheated, and had to stop. Sometimes I even say "whew."

"This time it's going to be different, though," I said out loud to myself, as I tried to get my confidence up. I wandered from the refreshment table to the penguin display. "Tonight I really *am* going to dance." I still hadn't figured out how I was going to get my nerve up, or who I was going to ask. All I knew was that somehow, before the night was over, it had to happen. It just *had* to.

All of a sudden, I felt someone tap me on the shoulder. I spun around to look, but there was no one there.

"Down here," said a giggling voice.

I looked down and saw B. B. Appleton. B. B. Appleton is the shortest boy in the entire seventh grade. I hate to make fun of someone's height, but if he had been wearing a tuxedo, he could have passed for a penguin.

"Dance?" asked B.B., starting to laugh.

I looked around behind me. "Are you talking to me?" I asked finally.

B.B. didn't answer. Instead, he just grabbed my hand and pulled me to the edge of the dance floor. "Come on," he giggled. "We'll miss the record."

Then, before I knew what happened, B.B. put his little arms around my waist and began trying to steer me around the floor. He didn't even wait for me to bend down.

At first, I didn't know what to do. Slow dancing with someone so short made me feel like a carnival act. Quickly, I hunched over as far as I could, but it didn't really help. When I looked down, I could still see the entire top of B.B.'s head. A small spitball was sitting in his hair.

Seeing the spitball didn't surprise me. B. B. Appleton's the kind of kid who's really into spitballs and stuff like that. If my grandmother knew him she'd probably call him a little imp. An imp is a kid who's in trouble a lot, but is cute enough to get away with it.

As the record went on, I was surprised to find that I didn't hate dancing with B.B. as much as I thought I would. He giggled a lot, but I figured it was probably just nerves. And even though he was short, at least his shirt was buttoned. Besides, since both of us had a problem with our height, I sort of felt that we understood each other. B.B. must have thought so, too. Why else would he have chosen me over the shorter girls?

Suddenly, it hit me all at once. B. B. Appleton had actually *asked* me to dance. And if a shrimp like B.B. wanted to dance with me, then maybe some of the taller boys wouldn't mind either. Maybe boys even *liked* dancing with tall girls! We might be easier to steer or something. The thought almost made me laugh out loud. My wish had come true. It had really come true!

After the record was finally over, B.B. and I hurried off in different directions. Drew was standing alone at the refreshment table looking humiliated. She said that while she and Ernest had been dancing, his shirt had fallen off his shoulders.

I didn't tell her about my dance with B. B. Appleton. B.B.'s not really one of Drew's favorite people. He stole a couple of Twinkies out of her lunch sack during the beginning of the year and she thinks he's a jerk.

For the rest of the night, Drew and I spent most of our time going from the refreshment table to the girls' room. One time, I thought about asking B.B. to fast dance. But when I finally spotted him, he was throwing pretzels, so I didn't want to bother him. It didn't really matter. The important thing was that I almost had the nerve to try.

The dance ended at ten o'clock. Drew and Belinda stayed in the gym while I went outside to call my mom. As usual, by the time I reached the phone booth there was already a bunch of kids in front of me, so I slipped quietly in line to wait my turn.

Suddenly, a few feet in front of me, two boys began shoving each other around. One was Ralph Mahoney. The other one was so short I couldn't see his head, so I knew right away it was B. B. Appleton.

"Come on," said Ralph, trying to grab something out of B.B.'s hand. "Just let me see it for a second. I just want to see if it's real."

B.B. held his little hand out. "It's real, all right," he replied. "Look. A five dollar bill, just like I told you."

Ralph examined the money and handed it back. "How'd you get it?" he asked suspiciously. "What'd you do, rip somebody off?"

B.B. looked insulted and shook his head. "I earned every penny of it," he said proudly. "Just ask Harold Dunbar if you don't believe me. He's the one who gave it to me."

"Gave it to you for what?" asked Ralph curiously. "What'd you have to do to get it?"

B.B. made a face and laughed meanly. "I had to dance with Beanpole."

8

Gloomy Gus

For the next few weeks, I spent most of my free time in my room more depressed than I've ever been in my life. I knew I should try to forget about what I had heard at the dance, but I just couldn't. Every time I closed my eyes, I could still see B.B. holding up his five dollars and laughing.

After the second week, my mother began to wonder what was wrong with me. Every time she walked by my door, she'd mumble something about how a growing girl needs fresh air and exercise.

"Thanks anyway, but I prefer my air stale," I would reply, but softly enough so that she didn't hear.

Besides, she didn't know it but I *was* getting exercise. Every so often, I would pull myself off my bed and do a couple of short pom-pom routines. I've had a set of purple and yellow pom-poms for several years now, and whenever I get depressed, I get them off my bulletin board and swish them around the room. I can't really explain it, but for some reason, picturing myself as a real life pom-pom girl has always given me hope that someday I can lead a normal life.

Still, even with pom-poms, it was hard to snap out of my depression. And it wasn't long before Drew and Belinda began to suspect that something was wrong. I still went to school and everything, but I got it over with as fast as I could. I got there in the morning just as the bell rang, and left promptly at three. At lunch, I kept getting indigestion from eating my sandwich in four bites. Then, I'd excuse myself so I didn't have to sit there and talk. Drew was worried about me. She thought that I was becoming hyperactive, and suggested that I go out for the girls' track team to work off my nervous energy. Belinda simply thought I was hungry.

Finally, to get them both off my back, I told them I was probably just hitting another growth spurt. "Getting to be eight feet tall really works up quite an appetite," I muttered quietly as I got up from the table. I made it to the hall before they could see my tears.

Christmas vacation was a real dud. I got so sick of people acting merry, I thought I was going to scream. Christmas day was the worst. I tried to act happy, but I'm just not very good at faking smiles. My mother kept asking if I had an upset stomach. I opened my presents in the morning and then went back to bed. Mom and Dad gave me clothes. All the pants were too short. Aunt Millie sent me a set of nontoxic zoo animals.

By the time vacation was over, my mother had grown very impatient with my unsociable behavior. She tried having a few mother-daughter chats, but whenever she asked me anything, I just shrugged my shoulders and hummed, "I don't know." When you hum "I don't know," you make your voice go up and down without really saying the words. My mother really hates it when I do that. She doesn't know what to do. I found a book in her room called *How to Talk to Your Teen,* but I don't think they covered humming.

Sometimes, I just wish adults would understand there are some things you don't want to talk about—and that's that. After the dance, it was bad enough knowing that I was the biggest freak in the world without sitting on my bed chatting with my mother about it. And no matter what, I knew I could never bring myself to admit that someone had actually been paid five dollars to dance with me. Never in a million years.

Mostly, the only thing I *could* bring myself to say was, "I'm not hungry." And eventually, my mother got just as mad about that as she did about my humming.

It was a Sunday, the fourth weekend since the dance, and it seemed that all she had been doing lately was calling me to meals. It was really starting to get on my nerves. "I *said*, I'm not hungry!" I shouted through the door for the umpteenth time.

If someone is upset enough to spend four solid weeks in her room, chances are she probably doesn't have much of an appetite. You'd think even a parent could figure that one out.

"Lillian!" yelled my mother, standing outside my bedroom door. "This may come as a shock to you, but I didn't ask you whether or not you were hungry. If I had wanted to know if you were hungry, it would have sounded something like this: 'Lillian, are you hungry?' But it didn't sound like that, did it? Because what I said was *'Come to dinner!'* Now, let's go. I don't know what your problem is lately because you refuse to talk about it. But I do know that your grandparents are here for Sunday dinner and you are expected at the table in two minutes! If I had wanted to raise a hermit crab, I would have bought one!"

I didn't bother to argue with her any further. I could tell by her voice that she meant business.

Needless to say, dinner that night was a disaster. It was obvious that my mother had told my grandparents about my recent behavior. I could see Grandma Woo-Woo's little eyes light up as soon as I sat down, and right away I had the feeling that I was in for another Ugly Duckling story. I know my grandmother means well, but for some reason she seems to think that every problem in my life can somehow be solved by telling me about that icky little swan.

"If I've said it once, I've said it a thousand times," she said, beaming. "Even though things may not look too good for you today, tomorrow you may wake up as a beautiful swan with all your problems behind you."

For a second, no one said anything. I think we all felt a little embarrassed for her. But Grandma Woo-Woo didn't seem to notice. She just sat there looking all around the table as if she were expecting applause or something.

Finally, my father broke the awkward silence. "What your grandmother is trying to say," he began, clearing his throat, "is that even though you might think you have problems, tomorrow something wonderful could happen and turn your life completely around. But you have to be ready for the good things to happen. And that means you can't go through life looking like a Gloomy Gus."

I rolled my eyes. I knew it would probably make him mad, and I was right. But I just couldn't help it. If there's one thing I hate, it's being called a Gloomy Gus.

"What your *father's* trying to say," interrupted my mother quickly before my father got a chance to yell at me, "is that when you're very young, sometimes problems seem much larger than they really are. And even though things may not be going your way today, there are many, many good times in store for you. And you just have to give them a chance. Take Pom Squad tryouts, for instance. Didn't you bring home an announcement that they were going to take place in a few weeks?"

She waited for an answer, so I bent my head in the direction of my potatoes.

"There, see?" she said excitedly. "You've been looking forward to trying out for the Pom Squad ever since you were in the fifth grade. And now it's finally going to happen! Isn't that something to be happy about?"

Everyone was silent, waiting for me to reply.

"Well?" prodded my mother. "Isn't it?"

I didn't want to talk about it, but they were forcing me. Why couldn't they just leave me alone?

"Lillian! Answer your mother!" snapped my father, still mad about me rolling my eyes.

Quickly, I stood up and pushed my chair away from the table. "Okay. I'll answer her," I said much too loudly. "No, Mother. No. It's nothing to be happy about. How can I be happy about Pom Squad tryouts when I'm not even trying out? Did everyone hear that? I, Lillian 'The Giant' Pinkerton, am not trying out for Pom Squad. Not this year, not next year, not ever! Now, if I can be excused, I think I'll go back to my room and try to keep myself from turning into a swan. Right now, that's *all* I'd need!"

No one excused me, but I left the table anyway and ran back to my room. Once I was safely inside, I locked the door and threw myself on the bed. I know that throwing myself on the bed sounds a little dramatic, but that's how I felt. Then, I started to sob into my pillow.

There! I thought to myself. I hope they're satisfied! Just when I was almost over the dance, they had to go and make me tell them I'll never be able to try out for the Pom Squad!

To me, the eighth grade Pom Squad is the neatest organization in the whole school. The cheerleaders are neat, too. But to be a cheerleader you have to know how to do a flip, and that let me out completely. Anytime I'm upside down, my legs get tangled up. In Pom Squad, though, you're never upside down. Instead of doing flips, you do precision pom-pom routines to music during basketball games and school assemblies.

Ever since I had received the tryout announcement, I had tried to put it out of my mind. But now, I had to face the fact that I would never be one of the girls in the cute blue and gold uniforms. How could a giant freak like me ever even hope to have a chance of making the squad? The answer was simple. There *was* no chance. And there was no sense humiliating myself by trying.

I was so disappointed, I could hardly stand it. My mother said I had wanted to try out for the Pom Squad since the fifth grade, but it was long before that. Actually, I had had dreams about it ever since Cindy Brinkley's birthday party in kindergarten. I was sitting on the floor of her living room with all the other kids watching her open presents when her mother brought out a large package from her aunt in Philadelphia. I remember it was from Philadelphia because when she opened the box, there were two giant green and silver pom-poms from the Philadelphia Eagles football team.

Cindy grabbed them out of the box and started swishing them wildly around the room like a big shot. Some of the streamers ripped off, and I picked them up and stuck them down in my sock. I figured maybe I could use them to make my own pom-poms when I got home.

Finally Mrs. Brinkley made her put them back in the box and called us all in the kitchen for ice cream and cake. I didn't go, though. Instead, I waited for everyone else to leave and then snuck over and pulled the pom-poms back out of the box. After I had gotten the feel of them, I started strutting around the room, singing to myself and pretending there was a big band marching behind me. Every once in a while, I jumped high in the air, shaking the pom-poms over my head and giggling.

I was having such a good time, I hardly even noticed Mrs. Brinkley coming back into the living room after me. She didn't say anything. She just removed the pom-poms from my hands and led me into the kitchen with the others. I really felt like a nitwit.

Remembering made me even more upset than

before. "I'm never coming out of here! Never!" I screamed into my pillow. "And I'm never eating another Sunday dinner, or going to another disgusting dance, or looking at another pom-pom as long as I live!"

9

Pros vs. Cons

I heard someone tapping at my bedroom door and looked at the clock. It had been almost an hour since I had left the table.

"Please go away," I said as nicely as I could. "I really just want to be alone."

The tapping continued.

"I *said*, please, go away."

Tap . . . tap . . . tap . . . tap . . . tap . . . tap . . . tap . . . The noise was really beginning to get on my nerves, and it was obvious that it wasn't going to stop until I opened up. Also, it was making me a little curious. Angry, I stormed over to the door, unlocked the handle, and hurried back to my bed.

Slowly, the knob turned and the door opened a crack. Trying to pretend I wasn't interested, I watched out of the corner of my eye as the door swung wider and a small black wing appeared near the floor and began to wave. It belonged to one of my penguins. Naturally, I had too much dignity to wave back, but right away, I knew it was my granddad crouching in the hall, working the little flipper.

Whenever I've been upset about something, ever since I was little, Granddad had always seemed to be able to find a way to cheer me up. When I had my tonsils out, for instance, I was the only kid in the hospital whose grandfather made her a tonsil puppet. It was just an old pink sock with eyes on it, but it talked to me about my operation and made me feel better. I loved him for it. This time, though, he was just wasting his time.

"No offense, Granddad," I muttered quietly, "but there are some things that a waving penguin just won't fix."

My grandfather put the penguin down and smiled sadly. "Too old for old Grandpop's little tricks, eh?"

The disappointment in his eyes made me feel even worse. Tears began to run down my cheeks. "I don't *want* to get older, Granddad. I really don't. Things were so much easier before I started to grow. Why does everything have to be so hard?"

My grandfather closed the door and walked over to my bed. When he sat down, I felt his hand reach out and smooth the back of my hair. I love my Granddad's hands. They're usually covered with paint splatters, but they always seem to know just where to pat.

"Growing up is always hard," he said gently. "Really it is. What you're feeling is very normal."

"Normal?" I sputtered. "Have you taken a good look at me lately? There's nothing normal about me! I look like a giant redwood! I'm a freak . . . a big, giant freak . . . and that's all there is to it. How can Mom and Dad even *think* about letting me try out for Pom Squad? If they had any feelings at all, you'd think they'd want to keep me home and hide me so that no one would make fun of me anymore. Even the Elephant Man got to wear a big brown blanket over his head."

My grandfather smiled understandingly and leaned down to give me a hug. Then, he took a big white handkerchief out of his shirt pocket and began dabbing the tears from my face. "Your mother and father are worried about you, Lillian," he said quietly. "They want you to be happy. And when you're young, part of that happiness is found by getting involved with your friends and school."

"I'm *not* going out for Pom Squad, Granddad!

I'm just not! And no one can make me! Not even you! There are too many reasons why I can't!"

"Whoa there. Slow down," he said, surprised at my outburst. "No one's going to try to make you, honey. You don't have to do anything you don't want to do. I want you to remember that."

I looked at him through a new set of tears and sniffled. "I don't?"

He shook his head and patted my hand. "Never," he assured me. "I promise."

Hearing his promise made me very relieved. "Tell Mom and Dad, okay? They'll listen to you."

"They'll listen to you, too, Lillian," he replied in a low, gentle voice. "It's just that sometimes they want things for you so badly, they have a hard time understanding why you don't want the same things for yourself. Take this Pom Squad thing, for example. I really just think they need your feelings on the matter, well, spelled out a little clearer, that's all."

"What'd you mean, 'spelled out clearer'?" I sniffed.

"I mean, why not make it crystal clear for them?" he continued. "Why not write it down on paper? List all the pros and cons of trying out for the squad. Write the good things as well as the bad. That way, when your parents see how much longer the 'bad' side is, it'll be easier for them to understand why you don't want to try out. Make sense?"

I had to admit, it did. If writing down my reasons would get my parents off my back, then it was definitely worth a try. I went to my desk and grabbed a sheet of paper and a pencil. Sometimes, I wish Granddad were a girl my own age. I'm sure we'd be best friends.

Granddad took my paper. "Okay," he said. "Let's get started. You do the thinking . . . I'll do the writing. Why don't we begin with the hard part. I know this won't be easy, but try to give me at least one good reason why you'd *like* to try out for the squad."

I thought for a minute and then shook my head and sighed. "I don't know, Granddad," I said finally. "All I can really think of is that the uniforms are sort of okay-looking. Will that do?"

Granddad nodded and next to number one wrote OKAY UNIFORMS.

"Nothing else?" he questioned.

"How many do you need?"

My grandfather shrugged his shoulders. "It's up to you."

"I don't know. I guess I should have enough to make it seem like I tried to be fair. Otherwise, Mom and Dad will say that I'm just being one-sided. Why don't you put down that being on the squad makes you seem kind of popular. At least that's what Belinda's always saying. Personally, I just think it would be sort of fun to ride the bus to all the basketball games."

Granddad wrote BE POPULAR and RIDE BUS next to numbers two and three. "Anything else?"

"Not really," I said reluctantly. "All my friends are trying out, I guess. At least Drew and Belinda are. I think Drew has even started exercising. She told me that her legs were so sore, she's been thinking about buying a cane."

Granddad chuckled.

"Belinda's even worse," I continued. "The Pom Squad gets their picture on the cover of the yearbook, and she's already talking about getting her hair frizzed so it'll go with her pom-poms. She says she read hair should match your outfit."

Granddad shook his head and finished writing FRIENDS. Then, he added YEARBOOK PICTURE. "That's five," he announced. "Any more?"

I shook my head. "Five's plenty. Now let's get to the reasons *against* trying out. Get ready to write. I've got at least a million of them."

"Shoot," said Granddad, his pencil up and ready to go.

"The first one's simple. I'm a giant freak."

My grandfather looked up and smiled. "Good one," he said, quickly writing it down.

In a way, it sort of surprised me. He didn't even try to talk me out of it. It just proved how different he was from my parents. They really have a fit when I call myself names.

Granddad penciled GIANT FREAK in big bold letters next to number one. "Next?" he called eagerly.

I hesitated before I went on, staring at the two large words in front of me. Seeing them there made me feel like Frankenstein or something. And after all, I might be tall, but at least my head's not shaped like a shoe box.

"Wait a minute, Granddad," I said at last. "Maybe *giant freak* sounds a little too dramatic. I mean, you and I know I'm a freak, but I'm really afraid if Mom and Dad saw it written down on my list, they'd sit me right down and give me their 'Tall Is Beautiful,' lecture. You know, it's the speech they made up for me when I was a maypole.

"Besides," I continued, "I've got a better one. I've never really told anyone this before, but the idea of tryouts makes me so nervous, I can hardly stand it. I mean, what if I had a heart attack right in the middle of the floor or something? I can just see me standing there in line and then suddenly keeling over like a big tree. And even if I didn't . . . just think how awful I'd feel if I went through all of that nervousness and then didn't make it. I'd die, Granddad! I'd absolutely *die!*"

My grandfather erased GIANT FREAK and started to write again. I watched carefully. Next to number one, he printed HEART ATTACK; next to two: DEATH.

I shook my head. "No offense again, Granddad," I said finally, "but do you think that maybe you could word it a little differently? *Heart attack* and *death* sort of make me sound like I'm ready for a nursing home or something."

Granddad gave the matter some thought and then started erasing again. "How about if we just put that you're scared you won't make it? How does that sound?"

I shrugged. It wasn't exactly what I had in mind, but at least it was better than *death*.

"You know, I probably wouldn't even like the stupid Pom Squad, anyway," I blurted. "The pom-poms they use aren't the best, you know. Belinda said she saw them in a box in the gym and they were sort of limp and the box smelled like mildew."

My grandfather's eyes lit up. Next to number two, he wrote STINKY DROOPY POMS.

I rolled my eyes. It looked even stupider than *giant*

freak. I think Granddad was beginning to sense my annoyance. After a minute, he put his pencil down and stood up.

"I think we're both getting a little tired, honey," he said softly. "Anyway, we don't need to finish it tonight. Why don't you just think about it for a while and look at it again in the morning?"

Then, he walked to the door and smiled. "Sometimes, the answers are right before our eyes and we're just too tired to see them. I bet things will look a lot clearer tomorrow."

After he left my room that night, I went straight to bed. I didn't even say good night to anyone. Drew says that no matter how mad you are, you should always make up with everyone before you go to sleep. She says, that way, if someone dies in the night, you won't feel like it's your fault. Drew can be a very morbid person.

10

Trying Out?

As it turned out, my grandfather was right. When I awoke the next morning and read my lists over a few times, I really *did* see things clearer. A *lot* clearer. As a matter of fact, it hardly took any time at all for me to figure out that he had been trying to trick me. The more I thought about it, the more I knew I was right. By getting me to make two lists, Granddad was hoping that I would see all the good reasons in *favor* of the Pom Squad and change my mind about trying out. Why else would the "pros" be so long, and the "cons" so short?

It's called psychology. You tell a person you want

them to do one thing, when really you're trying to get them to do just the opposite. It's just an adult way of tricking you. When you're little, you get tonsil puppets; when you're older, you get psychology.

At first, I was furious. I really felt betrayed. "How could he do this to me?" I asked myself in disbelief. "How could he pretend that he was trying to be on my side, when all the time he was really on theirs?" I felt so hurt, I didn't even bother to get dressed. Instead, I yanked my robe out of the closet and headed right for the kitchen phone to call Granddad and give him a piece of my mind.

I never made it, though. In my rush to the door, I tripped over my penguin. It rolled over into my open closet and lay there on its back staring up at me. In a way, it was kind of spooky. It was almost like it was trying to keep me from going.

I stared back. And as I did, I couldn't help remembering the way Granddad had been crouched in the hall the night before, trying to work its little flipper . . . and how disappointed he had looked when I hadn't laughed. "Too old for old Grandpop's little tricks, eh?" he had said. And I don't think I've ever seen him look quite so sad.

I sat back down on my bed. I just couldn't do it. I couldn't call him up and tell him that another one of his tricks had failed. I know he deserved it. But his little tricks seemed so important to him, I just couldn't hurt his feelings like that again.

I put my head down on my pillow. A sick feeling began to spread over my entire body. If I wasn't going to hurt my grandfather's feelings, then that meant . . . I gulped hard . . . it meant I would have to go out for the Pom Squad after all.

I pulled the covers up over my head and tried not to throw up at the thought of it. "Okay, just calm down, Lillian," I said, attempting to get control of myself. "Just don't panic. Maybe there's another way out of this that you just haven't thought of yet. Maybe you could call Granddad tonight and tell him there was a huge pom-pom fire at school today and they've had to do away with the squad."

For a brief moment, I felt hopeful. But it faded fast. Because deep inside I knew that my grandfather was no dummy. And the only way he would be sure his trick had worked was if I actually showed up at tryouts.

"I can't! I just can't!" I shouted into my pillow. The sick feeling wouldn't go away. "I'm sorry, Granddad," I whimpered. "It's just asking too much. I care about your feelings. I really do. But I've got my own to look out for, too, you know."

I got off the bed and started to get dressed. I bent

down to get my shoes from the closet. The penguin was lying on top of one of my loafers. When I picked him up, he waved his little flipper. It was more than I could take.

"Oh, okay!" I shouted angrily. "You win! You *all* win! But I just hope you guys know what you're doing. Because I'm telling you right now: If anyone yells 'Timber' as I'm starting to keel over, I'll never forgive *any* of you. Never!"

Once I had finally made the decision to try out, things gradually began to settle back to normal for me. At school, I stopped wolfing down my food, which took Drew and Belinda by surprise.

"Gee," said Belinda, "I can't believe your growth spurt's over already. Can you, Drew?"

Drew rolled her eyes. I had a feeling she never fell for the whole story in the first place, and by the look on her face, I knew I was right.

"How much taller'd you get?" continued Belinda. "You don't look any taller, does she, Drew?"

Drew covered her head with her arms.

"Stand up next to her, Drew, and I'll see if you still come up to Lillian's shoulder."

Drew got up and left the table. Sometimes, when Belinda's being abnormally dense, Drew just can't seem to handle it.

Anyway, once Belinda got my growth spurt off her mind, most of the lunch-table talk for the next few weeks involved Pom Squad. Belinda announced that after much experimenting, she had finally found the perfect hairstyle for tryouts. She wouldn't tell us what it was, though. I think she was afraid that we would steal it.

I could tell by the way Drew kept limping that she was still practicing at home. I have a feeling it was the jumps that were really giving her trouble. I tried to call her one night, but Melanie told me she was squatting in the middle of the kitchen floor and she couldn't get up.

Sometimes, the three of us talked about practicing together, but we never got around to it. Deep inside, I don't think any of us really wanted to know who was best. It's more fun to look forward to something if you think you have a chance.

Tryouts were going to begin the second week in March. Since our school gets out at the end of May, they like to give the new Pom Squad a chance to get organized and practice together before the summer starts. I also think they practice a few times in August. That way, they're always ready to perform at the first assembly in September.

As the date of tryouts got closer I became more

and more nervous. Until finally, the night before they were to begin, I was so upset, I could hardly get to sleep. I knew that for the first few days we would probably just be learning the routines and stuff. But I still wasn't sure I could go through with it. The thought of standing in a line with the other girls and looking like a giant scared me to death. I could see it all now: LILLIAN KONG, tallest pom-pom girl in captivity. I tried to put it out of my mind and get some rest, but my eyes refused to close. The tighter I squeezed them, the more they fought to stay open.

At last, I just gave in and lay there staring at my ceiling. Would I have the nerve to try out or wouldn't I? I pulled the pillow around my head. "I don't know," I said out loud. "I just don't know if I can do it. If only I thought I had a chance . . . just a slim chance, it would make it so much easier. If only it were my birthday again, and I could make another wish. . . ."

My wishes—of course! The three wishes I had made at my party! All the candles had gone out but one. But did that *really* mean that only two wishes would come true? And even if it did, had both of them already been granted? I had a bra now. But I had begged so hard to get it, it really hadn't seemed very magical. And as for the second wish . . . was I really supposed to believe that being humiliated by B. B. Appleton was the same as getting to dance with a boy?

I thought about it for a long time. "No," I said at last, rolling my head from side to side on my pillow. There was no way in the world that dancing with B. B. Appleton could ever be considered a wish come true. No way. In the first place, I had requested a *boy,* not a dwarf. And in the second place, I had only said I wanted to *dance* with him, not build up his bank account. No, the whole thing had just been a mistake. A terrible, terrible mistake.

Anyway, if I was right about the dance, and it really *had* been a mistake, then that meant I still had at least one wish left to go. And maybe . . . just maybe, it meant that I still had a chance of making the Pom Squad after all. I took a deep breath. I just hoped that *this* time my wish-granter would be on her toes. "Better yet," I said out loud, "I just hope there *is* a wish-granter."

11

Hanging in There

My alarm went off at seven o'clock the next morning, and I felt like I had hardly slept at all. I forced myself out of bed and shuffled into the bathroom. I looked like something the cat dragged in. That's an expression my mother uses a lot. It means you look like a dead rodent.

When I got to school, Drew's eyes looked even worse than mine. It didn't really surprise me. When it comes to being smart, Drew's the most confident person I know. But when it comes to stuff like Pom Squad, she's a real worrier. We've never really talked about it, but I think it has something to do with her weight. Once, while we were playing Scrabble, she went home right after I spelled the word *plump*.

When I saw her in the hall that morning, I almost didn't recognize her. She doesn't get bags under her eyes like I do. Instead, hers puff up and look like little slits in her face.

The tryouts were supposed to take place after school in the faculty parking lot, but by the time three o'clock finally rolled around, my nerves were so bad I really didn't think I could make it. Also, the bags under my eyes were bigger, and I had started to get a headache. As a matter of fact, if Drew hadn't stopped by my locker, I probably would have headed right for home.

"Ready?" she said, trying to act casual as she peeked at me through her little slits. I looked her over closely and then nodded. I know it was mean, but even with my bags and headache, I figured I could still beat out poor Drew.

The two of us headed out to the parking lot. Belinda was already sitting on the curb waiting. After school she had frizzed her hair into two large ponytails. She called them ponytails pom-pom style.

"Hurry up, you two," she squealed excitedly when she saw us. "I saved you a seat. I wanted to make sure we got a good spot so we don't miss anything."

"God, Belinda, this isn't a parade," muttered

Drew. Sometimes, Drew gets a little annoyed with Belinda's carefree attitude. She says Belinda doesn't take life seriously enough.

After waiting outside for about fifteen minutes, the Pom Squad finally arrived in their cute little uniforms. They were followed by their faculty adviser, Mrs. Manly, the P.E. teacher. You could tell by the way they all pranced around, they really thought they were something special. The trouble was, so did I.

Mrs. Manly began pacing up and down with her arms behind her back explaining what being on the Pom Squad was all about. She said a bunch of stuff about school spirit and how you were supposed to be a credit to your uniform. It really gave me the creeps. She made me feel like I was joining the army.

When she was finished, Mrs. Manly asked for questions. Theresa Hartmond raised her hand and asked her if she had ever been in the marines. Theresa's one of those smart alecks teachers really hate, and Mrs. Manly was no exception. She just squinted at Theresa for a while like she was memorizing her face. I think it was her way of saying Theresa wouldn't be making the squad.

After the speech, we all lined up across the parking lot and began to learn the two pom routines we would have to do at the final tryouts. Altogether, there were forty-four of us. Mrs. Manly said that because of the large turnout, they would be making two cuts. In the first cut, they would narrow it down to fifteen finalists. And in the second, they would choose the eight winners. When she asked if there were any questions, a voice in the back asked if we should bring Band-Aids for the cuts. I'm pretty sure it was Theresa.

Once we finally got started, practice didn't make me as upset as I thought it would. There was so much confusion about the routines, no one even seemed to notice if you made a mistake. And best of all, I got to stand on the end, where I wasn't quite as noticeable.

Since there weren't nearly enough pom-poms to go around, Mrs. Manly said we would have to make fists and "just pretend." I really felt sorry for Drew. She got stuck next to Theresa Hartmond, and every time Theresa would fling her arms to the side, she would hit Drew in the stomach and say, "boom." It made Drew look a lot like a big, bass drum.

Practice lasted almost two hours. It was five thirty before Mrs. Manly said we could stop. She thanked us all for coming, and then handed out a sheet of paper with all the steps to the routines on them. She said next time we would meet in the gym and practice to music.

The Pom Squad members went back into the school to get out of their uniforms. The rest of us were told to go home and practice what we had learned. All except Theresa, that is. She was just told to go home.

Altogether, there were four more practices. Drew quit after the second one. That's when Lucy Lupton told her she looked like the Pillsbury Dough Boy. Drew pretended not to care, but I know she did. Her face went white as a biscuit, and she hurried home alone. The next day at school, she told me that she had decided to give up Pom Squad and "pursue" the flute.

I really felt sorry for her. If anyone knows anything about name-calling, it's me. I wanted to call Drew after school and tell her how much I understood. I wanted to tell her she shouldn't let a moron like Lucy ruin her chances of getting on the squad.

The trouble was, I wasn't sure what I should say. In the first place, I didn't want her to know that I had overheard what Lucy had said. It would have just been too humiliating for her. And in the second place, it was true. Drew really *does* look like the Pillsbury Dough Boy. One time for Halloween she went as a baker, and all night long, kids kept trying to poke her in the stomach to get her to giggle.

I decided to call anyway. Even if I said the wrong thing, at least she'd know I cared.

Drew picked up the phone on the fifth ring. "Hi," I said, trying to sound cheery. "You didn't wait for me after school again today. I was looking all over for you."

At first, Drew didn't reply. Then, I heard her blow her nose. "I just had to get home," she muttered finally, and it was plain to tell she was feeling terrible.

"You okay?" I asked quietly.

"You know, don't you?" she asked.

I hesitated a moment before deciding to answer. "You mean about Lucy?" I said at last. "Yeah, I know. I accidentally overheard her. What a jerk."

Except for a few more sniffles, Drew remained silent.

"Drew, you're not going to let this bother you, I hope. You're really not going to drop out because of an idiot like her, are you?"

Drew blew her nose again. "She can't be that much of an idiot," she mumbled softly. "She recognized me without my baker's suit, didn't she?"

"Stop it, Drew!" I ordered. "Stop it right now! Don't you know you can't let her do this to you? You've got to stand your ground and fight back, that's what you've got to do!"

I'd heard that line somewhere before, but I couldn't remember where. All I knew was that Drew had been very hurt, and I had to do something to help.

"Drew, are you listening to me? In the first place, you do not—I repeat—you do *not* look like the Pillsbury Dough Boy. And even if you did, so what? My grandmother says that Poppin' Fresh has the cutest smile of any other celebrity on TV."

"He's *not* a celebrity!" snapped Drew. "He's nothing but an overgrown fat little biscuit, and I really don't want to talk about it anymore!"

"Well, you *have* to talk about it," I insisted. "This really isn't like you, you know. Since when does brilliant Drew Clayton let some moron like Lucy Lupton get the best of her? Last month in social studies we had to do a report called My Most-Admired American, and do you know who Lucy picked? She picked Mickey Mouse, Drew. Mickey Mouse! She said he doesn't show his age and has a nice singing voice."

On the other end of the line, I could hear Drew begin to chuckle. "Thanks, Lillian," she said. "I needed that." As I laughed along with her I knew that she would be all right.

I still wasn't able to talk her into coming back to tryouts, though. She said that the flute was more "up her alley." And she seemed so relieved about not going back, I didn't really push it very much.

The good thing about having a big brain is that you're usually smart enough to know what you're good at and what you're not. And when it came to pom routines, Drew was definitely *not*. I think it had something to do with her timing. No matter how fast the routine was going, Drew always seemed to be going just a little bit faster. One time, I heard Mrs. Manly tell her there wasn't a prize for finishing first, but Drew just couldn't seem to control her speed.

When the first practices were finally over, Mrs. Manly made us all sit down while she gave another one of her speeches. This time, she told us that she was very proud that we had all "hung in there," and announced that the tryouts for the fifteen finalists would be held on the following Monday. She said the best advice she could give us would be to go home, get plenty of rest, and make sure we ate a healthy balanced diet and drank plenty of liquids. It was the same advice my doctor gave me when I had the measles, only the thought of finally being judged made me twice as sick.

12

Brenda

Saturday, Belinda invited me over to her house to practice. She said her mom had bought two new sets of pom-poms for us to work with. Belinda's mother is like that. It seems that almost every day when Belinda gets home, there's something new waiting for her on her bed. I think it's Mrs. Fischer's way of trying to stay in touch with her teenager. Every once in a while, my mother does the same thing. It's never anything neat, like pom-poms, though. Usually, it's three pairs of panties that were on sale at K Mart.

• When I got to Belinda's the next day, Mrs. Fischer opened the door. Mrs. Fischer is about the same age as my mother, but she tries to look a lot younger. Once, when I went shopping with them, she kept asking me if I thought she and Belinda could pass for sisters. Then, when we were eating lunch, she made me guess how old she was. I guessed thirty-seven. She was thirty-four. We left right after that, and I didn't even have a chance to finish my french fries.

Belinda was waiting for me in the living room with the pom-poms. I hadn't really expected that we would be practicing there. I just figured we'd be in the privacy of her room. Belinda's room is about four times as big as mine. It used to be the attic before they fixed it all up.

Mrs. Fischer disappeared for a minute, and Belinda handed me a set of the new pom-poms. Mrs. Fischer must have spent a fortune on them. They were the thickest ones I had ever seen. I almost couldn't find the end to hold them.

"Ready to get started?" asked Belinda eagerly.

"Here?" I questioned. "In the living room? Wouldn't it be better if we went up to your bedroom? What if your mother wants to watch TV or something in here?"

I know I was feeling better about trying out for

Pom Squad, but I still was feeling pretty self-conscious about having people watching me practice. Even my own mother hadn't seen me yet.

Belinda laughed. "Mom's not going to watch TV. She's going to watch *us,* silly."

I hate it when someone calls me silly, but before I had a chance to say anything else, Mrs. Fischer reappeared in the doorway. She had changed her clothes. She was wearing a cheerleading outfit.

"Ta daaaaa," she sang as she waltzed in. "How do you like it?"

Belinda giggled and started clapping her hands like mad. "You look great, Brenda! Really great!"

Belinda calls her mother by her first name. I don't know whose idea it was, but if you ask me, it's weird. I mean, I love my mother and everything, but to me she'll just never be "Doris."

"Brenda was a cheerleader in high school," explained Belinda, "and that's her old uniform. Can you believe how good she still looks in it? Isn't it just darling?"

All of a sudden, Mrs. Fischer spun around and began doing a cheer. At least I think it was a cheer. Mostly she just stamped her feet and made this hissing sound while she clapped. She reminded me of this witch doctor I saw once on a National Geographic special. When she had finished, Mrs. Fischer plopped down on the sofa and started fanning herself. Belinda began applauding even louder than before. "Wow, Brenda, that was great! Wasn't Brenda great, Lillian?"

I managed to nod.

"Okay, you two," said Mrs. Fischer, trying to catch her breath. "Now it's your turn. Let's see your stuff. Maybe I can give you a few pointers." She tossed her pom-poms to Belinda, and before I knew what was happening, Belinda had started the first routine.

I really felt like a fool. I smiled awkwardly at Mrs. Fischer and giggled nervously. She didn't smile back. She just made this hand motion for me to get started. I felt my face turning red, but I didn't know how to stop it.

"Whoa, whoa, whoa!" said Mrs. Fischer finally. "Hold it, hold it, hold it!"

"We're going to have to start over again," said Mrs. Fischer, frowning at me. "And *this* time, I want you both to start *together*. After all, Lillian ... I can't help you if I can't see your routine. Can I?"

Mrs. Fischer waited for a reply.

Nervously, I shrugged and shook my head at the same time.

"Okay, then," continued Mrs. Fischer, "let's take

it from the top. Ready? One . . . two . . . three . . . *begin*!"

While Belinda and I went through the steps to our pom routine, Mrs. Fischer sat on the couch and kept turning the edges of her mouth up with her fingers. I think that meant smile. I thought I would die.

When we were finally finished, Mrs. Fischer took her fingers off her mouth and clapped until her hands turned red.

"Hey! What's all the noise in here?" said a voice from the doorway. It was Mr. Fischer, or as Belinda calls him, Don.

Mrs. Fischer jumped up off the couch and did another "Ta daaaaaa." Mr. Fischer's eyes practically bulged right out of their sockets when he saw her in her old uniform. He hurried over and put his arms around her and hugged her right in front of us.

Mrs. Fischer's eyes kept peeking at me over her husband's shoulder. I didn't know where to look, so I just sort of stood there with this real dumb grin on my face.

Finally, Mr. Fischer stopped hugging his wife and looked her over again. "You're really amazing, you know it?" he said still holding her hands. "Just *look* at you in that uniform. You've *really* taken good care of yourself."

I felt like I was in the middle of a Geritol commercial.

Just then, Mr. Fischer turned to me and smiled. "How old would you say my wife is, Lillian? Just take a guess."

I felt myself start to sweat. This was the second chance I'd had at this question, and this time, I just *had* to get it right. Mrs. Fischer looked as worried as I did.

"Twenty-three!" I blurted suddenly. "She looks twenty-three!" I closed my eyes and prayed I was low enough to make everyone happy. When I opened them again, Mrs. Fischer looked very relieved. Mr. Fischer picked her up and twirled her around.

I was feeling more and more uncomfortable by the minute. "Listen," I said to Belinda. "I really feel bad about this, but I've got to go early. That's really what I came over here to tell you this morning. I mean your pom-poms are really great and everything, but my mom said we had to go somewhere today, so I'll probably just have to finish practicing at home."

"You mean you're going *now?*" asked Belinda, sounding disappointed. "After we finished practicing, Brenda was going to let us try on her uniform."

I tried to look unhappy. "Oh, darn," I replied.

"That's too bad. Maybe I could try it some other time."

Belinda walked me to the door. On the way, I waved to Mr. and Mrs. Fischer. They didn't see me, though. They were still busy twirling.

It was really a relief to get home. I know that sometimes my mother and I don't get along, but at least I don't have to guess her age every two minutes. When I walked in the door, Mom was in the living room watering her plants.

"Hi ya there, Doris," I cracked. "How's my best pal?"

My mother looked to make sure it was me. "Doris?" she mumbled quietly.

I smiled to myself and headed up to my room to practice.

13

The Cut

After school on Monday, I went into shock. It happened right after I found out I made the first cut.

Shock is what your body does when it's not prepared to handle unexpected news. Your ears hear the words being said, but the rest of you acts like it never happened. Sometimes, it can last for years. When Aunt Betty ran off with the paperboy, Grandma Woo-Woo went into shock and never totally recovered. Even after ten years, if someone mentions Uncle Rocky, Grandma says, "Rocky who?"

Since I don't really remember much about Monday afternoon, Belinda tried to fill me in on as many details as she could. She told me that when it came my turn to try out, I ran quickly to the middle of the gym, did my routine with five other girls, and then ran back to the bleachers and put my head between my legs.

Putting your head between your legs is a first-aid procedure against fainting. I think it's supposed to get blood to your brain in a hurry. Also, it keeps you all balled up so if you do pass out, you can just slump quietly to the floor and not call a lot of attention to yourself.

I guess I was still in my "faint" position when Mrs. Manly called out the names of the winners, so I didn't hear her call mine. Belinda was so excited, she began jumping up and down and pounding me on the back. I finally got annoyed and straightened up long enough to ask her to please be quiet so I could hear the winners.

"You *are* a winner!" she shouted. "They already picked you! You're in the finals!"

After that, the rest of the afternoon was a big blur. Belinda said that she finally got me to walk out to the middle of the gym floor, but I didn't jump around and hug everyone like the rest of the girls were doing. She told me I just stood there with this real weird grin on my face, and when one of the other girls came up and hugged me, I said, "Thank you." The good thing about being in shock is that you don't care if you're acting like a fool. Nothing bothers you. I think I should do it more often.

I didn't get home until after five that night. My mother greeted me at the door. I guess when she saw my face she figured that I had lost. She smiled. But it wasn't a happy smile. It was the kind of smile you give a person when her cat dies.

I tried to smile back, but I couldn't. Instead, I sat down on the couch and started staring at a piece of fuzz on the floor. I was really acting spooky. If I hadn't been in shock, I probably would have even spooked myself.

I think my mother was alarmed. She sat down next to me and put her arms around me. "I know you're disappointed, sweetie. But it's not the end of the world. *Everyone* has to lose sometimes."

I kept staring at the piece of fuzz. "I didn't," I replied at last.

"You didn't what, honey?" asked my mother quietly.

"I didn't lose."

"You didn't lose?"

"I made the cut."

"You made the cut?" My mother was beginning to sound a lot like a parrot.

"Frank!" she shouted to my father. "Lillian didn't lose! She made the cut! Lillian made the cut!"

My father came bounding in from the kitchen. I guess he was hiding in there in case I had come home sobbing and stuff. My father's not very good in sobbing situations. He usually just tries to pat you on the back until you stop. Sometimes, you stop sobbing just so he'll stop patting. This time, though, he didn't do any patting at all. Instead, he picked me up and spun me around until I started feeling sick. When he finally set me down, I fell over.

It wasn't until later that night that I finally began to realize what had happened to me. I think it started sinking in sometime between 11:30 and 12:00 A.M. "I can't believe it," I whispered to myself. "I just can't believe it. I'm a winner. A real, honest-to-goodness winner!"

Suddenly, I jumped out of bed and turned on my light. I did my pom routines in the mirror and hopped back into bed more excited than before.

"It's *not* a mistake!" I said, laughing. "It's not! I'm really good!" Just to be sure, I got up and did the routines again. Maybe it's finally happening, I thought. Maybe my life's beginning to change!

I studied myself in the mirror. My hair had now grown past my shoulders, and I casually shook it from side to side like the girl does in my favorite dandruff shampoo commercial. Was it really possible that at last I was putting my awkward beanpole days behind me? Were people finally going to stop saying, "Ho ho ho," in my ear and asking me if I had any lima beans in butter sauce?

I hurried down the hall to my parents' room and switched on their light. "I'm good! I'm really good!" I squealed, shaking my pom-poms and hugging them both.

My mother snarled groggily and covered her head with the pillow. My father just squinted and kept saying, "What the . . . ? What the . . . ?"

Finally, I turned off their light and went back to my room. This time I didn't want my eyes to close. Being a winner was the most wonderful thing that had ever happened to me. And I wanted to hang on to the feeling forever.

Drew and Belinda seemed really happy that I had made the finals. When Drew found out, she told me I deserved it. She said it was about time that "girls like us" had a chance to make the squad. I would have liked it a lot better if she hadn't said "girls like us," but I thanked her anyway.

Belinda didn't seem too upset that she hadn't made it herself. The next day, she was already busy making plans to get on the school newspaper. She heard they were running short of help and said she thought it was time they had a fashion editor. She had already decided to wear her hair in a bun like lady executives do. Also, her mother promised to buy her a necktie.

My grandparents sent me flowers. On the card, Granddad drew a little smiling penguin and wrote, *You're a winner!* Grandma Woo-Woo was so excited, she called her sister. Two days later, Aunt Millie sent me a talking dog in a cheerleader suit. When you pulled his chain, he said, "Sis Boom Bah." His voice was deeper than my dad's. It sounded a lot like the devil in *The Exorcist*. I haven't seen him since the day I got him because I started laughing so hard, my mother got mad and took him away.

The finals were going to be on Friday afternoon. Mrs. Manly told us we could use the extra few days to perfect our "pomming." I don't think "pomming" is a word, but I didn't say anything. Mrs. Manly is a P.E. teacher, and I don't think vocabulary is that important to her.

I took her advice and practiced my routines every spare minute I had. By Thursday, I could practically do them in my sleep. As a matter of fact, I knew them so well, I actually decided to try them in front of an audience. Sometimes, having people gawk at you is good experience.

My mother went a little bit nuts. As soon as I told her I'd like to show her my routines, she got right on the phone and invited my grandparents over for my big "performance." I guess I really couldn't blame her, though. It was the first time in my entire life that I had ever really agreed to put on a show for anyone.

Most little kids are always putting on shows. Drew used to do it all the time. At least once a week, she'd dress up in her mother's clothes and sing "People Who Need People" to anyone who'd listen. Not me, though. Even when I practiced the cello, I did it facing the wall. I *was* the maypole, of course, but that didn't count. In the first place, it wasn't my idea. And besides, being wrapped up in brown paper can't really be considered "performing."

Before I knew it, my mother was outside in the backyard setting up folding chairs. She told me I would have more space and freedom of expression out there. I took them down and said the living room would be just fine, but I don't think she heard me. She was too busy fixing cheese and crackers to pass around after the show.

My grandparents showed up at seven o'clock. I waited until everyone was seated before I came downstairs. I have to admit, when I saw them all grinning at me, I felt sort of foolish. But in a way,

I was really excited to show them that finally, after all these years, I was actually *good* at something. Sometimes, I think I've been a disappointment for Mom and Dad. Raising a tall, shy kid with no talent is probably about as thrilling as raising a celery stick.

Before I began, I explained that my pom-poms were pretty old, but at least everyone could get the general idea. My grandfather frowned. Then, he took a ten-dollar bill out of his pocket and stuffed it into my father's hand. "For heaven's sake, Frank, get the girl some decent pom-poms." My father rolled his eyes.

I hurried to get started. I went through both routines without stopping. No one pointed to their mouths and told me to smile. When I was finished, Grandma Woo-Woo had tears in her eyes. She told me when I did my jumps at the end, I leaped like a swan. I didn't want to hurt her feelings, but I don't really think swans do a lot of leaping. Still, it was nice of her to cry.

Everyone else just started clapping and hugging . . . clapping and hugging. My parents really looked proud. Mom said I had the highest jump she had ever seen. Then, she and my father started arguing over which side of the family gave me my spring.

The thing is, I *knew* where I got my spring. I got it by hard work and practice. And because of all my effort, I was actually beginning to think I could make it. In fact, I practically *knew* I could. And it was the best feeling in the world.

That night, when I went to bed, I couldn't believe how good I felt. I was very nervous, of course. But it was a *good* kind of nervous . . . not the worrying kind that makes you feel sick. Even thinking about my height didn't bother me much. After all, I had made it to the finals being tall, and I was pretty sure I hadn't grown much since Monday.

Smiling to myself, I pulled the covers up around my shoulders and closed my eyes. "Just in case there really *is* a wish-granter up there listening," I whispered, "this is Lillian Pinkerton. And, I just wanted to say that I don't think I'll be needing you tomorrow. I mean, I really think I can handle this one on my own. I know now that it takes a lot more than wishing to make my dreams come true. It takes hard work and determination. And I happen to have them both!"

I opened my eyes and sighed. Then, after thinking it over a minute, I closed them again. "However . . . just in case you happen to be in the neighborhood, I'll be in the junior high gym at three. . . ."

14

The Finals

"Clancy, Hager, Royal, Green, and Gardner!"

The first group of five finalists ran to the middle of the gym floor and waited for Mrs. Manly to start the music to the routine. This was it: my very first finals, and you could almost feel the nervousness in the room. Everywhere you looked, people were sitting around taking deep breaths.

I studied the girls around me and the ones already waiting to begin. Seven of us would be going home losers. Eight would be winners. I swallowed hard. I had to be one of the eight. I just *had* to be.

Suddenly, the music began and the first five started off the competition. Clancy and Hager looked the most nervous. When they tried to smile, their mouths were so dry their lips kept sticking to their gums. Green's smile wasn't much better. It didn't seem to be dry, but it quivered a lot. You could see the twitching from the bleachers.

Gardner and Royal were the best. I kept waiting for them to goof up, but neither one of them made a mistake. It was really disappointing. My parents say that someday I'll realize that it's better to lose fairly than to win because of another person's misfortune. But right now, I'm still young enough to wish that everyone else will fall down.

As soon as group number one was finished, Mrs. Manly looked down at her paper and blared out five more names. *"Smith, Swenson, Bendix, Ritter, and Flowers!"*

She sounded like a drill sergeant. The first group hardly had time to run off the floor before she started the music for the second one. Poor Smith didn't make it to her position in time. She was hurrying so fast to get there that she tripped, dropped a pom-pom, and fell down. That's when her retainer fell out of her mouth. You'd think that Mrs. Manly would have been nice enough to stop the record and let her start over. She wasn't, though. Smith had to do her whole routine holding one pom-pom and one retainer.

Out of all the contestants I had seen so far, I felt sorriest for Bendix and Ritter. Halfway through the second routine, they got the giggles. It was the kind of laughing where nothing is really funny, but you just can't seem to control yourself. I think it's caused by nerves. I could tell that Mrs. Manly was really disgusted with them. I saw her draw a big black mark through their names. One time she had told us that we should have a good time, but *too* much fun would not be tolerated.

Out of the second group, Flowers was definitely the best. Swenson was good, too, but she was wearing a ton of make-up. She looked about forty. I don't think Mrs. Manly goes in much for that sort of thing. Judging from her appearance, she goes in more for the "natural" look.

"Palumbo, Canter, Franklin, Gillette, and Pinkerton!"

I took a deep breath and stood up. My legs felt like jello. I just prayed that they could hold me up until after I had finished my routines. I got to the middle of the gym floor just as Mrs. Manly started the record. I didn't even have time to think. Immediately, I started the first routine.

Next to me, I heard Paula Sue Palumbo start to panic. "Step, step, turn . . . step, two-three-four . . . turn, turn, turn," she muttered as she desperately tried to remember the steps to the routine. Suddenly, I heard her groan. She had turned the wrong direction and couldn't figure out how to get back around. I really felt sorry for her. She ended up doing the first routine facing the wall.

Besides Paula Sue, I couldn't tell how the rest of my group was doing. I was on the end, so I couldn't see much. It was all I could do to concentrate on my *own* routine. Paula Sue had started to whimper a lot, and it was very distracting.

Finally, the music stopped. I ran back to the bleachers as fast as my jello would carry me. As soon as I sat down, Flowers patted me on the back and said, "good job." It was nice, but it would have meant a lot more if she hadn't said the same thing to Paula Sue.

Mrs. Manly didn't waste any time. She excused herself from the room and said she would be back in a few minutes with the results. The regular members of the Pom Squad followed her into the girls' locker room. I thought I saw one of them point at me before she left, but I couldn't be sure. The only thing I was sure of was that I had done my best. I had gone through both routines without one mistake. I know I hadn't smiled much, but after seeing what had happened to the others' smiles, I just couldn't risk it.

As I sat there, I checked out the other girls in my group. Canter and Franklin both looked pretty relaxed. I wondered if that meant that they had done well. Gillette was busy trying to console Palumbo. She told her that doing the routine backward made it look like she had a good sense of humor.

It seemed like Mrs. Manly was gone for hours. But according to the clock, it was only fifteen minutes. Palumbo didn't bother waiting for the results. She said she was going home to throw up. Suddenly, Mrs. Manly and the Pom Squad reappeared in the doorway. All talking stopped. You could almost hear the hearts beating around you.

Mrs. Manly walked to the center of the floor and took out a piece of paper. "We have our winners," she said seriously as she gazed at the sheet in front of her. The gym was so quiet, you could have heard a pin drop. "But first," she continued, "before I announce their names, I would like to say a few words to the losers."

Everyone in the bleachers moaned at once, but Mrs. Manly pretended not to notice. Instead, she started spouting off this ridiculous speech on how wonderful we all were, and how it was "better to have tried and lost, than never to have tried at all."

I hate that! Every time you lose at something, grown-ups spend hours trying to tell you how happy you should be about it. If they're *that* concerned about my happiness, why don't they just pick me to win in the first place?

Finally, Gillette couldn't stand it anymore and raised her hand. "No offense, Mrs. Manly," she said, "but if you don't tell us the names of the winners soon, I think I'm going to wet my pants."

Mrs. Manly glared at her for a minute, but finally she took the paper and held it out in front of her. "Okay, everyone," she said. "I'd now like to introduce the members of next year's Pom Squad. If you hear your name called, please go to the locker room and pick up your pom-poms."

The tension started to get to me. Immediately, I went into my faint position. I figured either way, it couldn't hurt.

During the next few minutes, there was more screaming and yelling than I've ever heard in my life. Also crying. Some of the girls didn't think losing was as much fun as Mrs. Manly said it should be.

When the confusion died down, there were eight happy girls in the locker room getting their pom-poms. Six others had gone home.

One remained in the bleachers. She was still in the faint position.

She was me.

● ● ●

I'm not sure how long I sat there like that. It must have been pretty long, though. The gym was quiet for a while, and then someone poked me on the arm and told me to "git."

I looked up and saw Mr. Trumble, the custodian.

"Git?" I repeated.

"Go on . . . git," he growled. "I've gotta lock up." Mr. Trumble is probably the meanest janitor in the world. Also the rudest. The least he could have done was say "*please* git."

Annoyed, I climbed down from the bleachers and headed toward the door. Mr. Trumble was pointing at it with his mop.

"Git, yourself," I said as I passed him. I don't usually talk back to adults, but Mr. Trumble deserved it. I hope he never makes head janitor.

Maybe if I had been crying, Mr. Trumble would have been nicer. But there were so many things going through my head, I guess I just didn't have enough room left over for tears. Why hadn't I made it? What had gone wrong? I had practiced so hard. I had been so careful. It just wasn't fair. After all, *I* wasn't the one who got my lips caught on my gums or made a wrong turn. I deserved to win. So what had gone wrong?

I shook my head in confusion. "And just when I was getting to feel almost normal, too," I mumbled sadly. Maybe Drew had been right. Maybe "girls like us" just didn't stand a chance. No matter how hard I tried, maybe giants like me could never really belong.

As I closed the door to the gym, I saw Mrs. Manly getting into her car to go home. I guess when I saw her, I must have gone a little bit crazy. Without even thinking about it, my legs rushed me over to her car. When Mrs. Manly saw me coming, she hurried to roll up her window. I guess she thought I was going to try to choke her or something.

I motioned for her to roll it back down. Reluctantly, she opened it a crack and put her mouth near the opening.

"Yes?"

"Was it because I was too tall?" I blurted, leaning closer. "Is that why you didn't pick me?"

Mrs. Manly looked really disgusted. I thought she was going to roll the window back up on my lips. Instead, she took a deep breath and rested her head on the steering wheel for a minute.

"For your information, Pinkerton," she began finally, "I do *not* judge people on how tall or short they are. I happen to judge them on their performance. And if you had listened to anything I said today, you would know that *all* the girls . . . and that includes you . . . did a terrific job today." Then, she paused a minute. "Except, of course, those two nitwits who couldn't stop laughing."

"But if I was good, then . . ."

Mrs. Manly didn't wait for me to finish. "I could only pick eight, Pinkerton," she interrupted. "And I had to go with the eight girls that I thought did just a little bit better than everyone else. You were good, Pink, you were very good . . . maybe if you had smiled more. I don't know. Why don't you practice your smile and try out again in high school?" Then, without waiting for an answer, she rolled up her window and sped off.

For a moment, I just stood there. My mind was more confused than ever. I thought I would be relieved knowing that I hadn't lost because of my height. I wasn't, though. I was too annoyed to feel anything but anger. What was it she had said? "Practice your smile and try again in high school?" What's wrong with grown-ups, anyway? Don't they know that to a seventh grader, high school seems like forever? And besides, how in the world do you practice a smile? "What am I supposed to do," I muttered, "stand in front of my mirror and grin at myself for two years?"

Mrs. Manly's car was almost out of view. Angrily, I raised my fists in the air. *"And don't call me Pink!"* I shouted after her.

Slowly, I turned and started for home. I really took my time. I knew as soon as I hit the door I'd probably start blubbering, so it wasn't the sort of thing you want to rush right home to. Also, I knew that everyone there would be anxiously awaiting the news, and I just didn't think I was up to it.

15

More Than a Loser

As I rounded the corner to my street, I saw my grandparents' car sitting in front of my house. My mother was stationed outside, acting as lookout. She was pretending to sweep the sidewalk, but it didn't fool me a bit. My mother hasn't swept the sidewalk in ten years.

As I walked toward her, she stopped sweeping and looked up. I guess the look on my face told the whole story. She didn't even bother to ask. Instead, she reached out and touched my sleeve as I passed. "I'm sorry, honey," she said quietly. Then, she pretended to sweep some more.

I knew my grandparents were waiting in the living room, but I just couldn't face them. I ran straight upstairs to my room and flopped down on my bed. This was it. There was nothing left to do but cry.

I waited. But nothing happened. I waited some more. Then, after a few more minutes, I tried to force a few small whimpers. Still, no tears. I began to get frustrated. If you don't cry when you lose at something, it makes it seem like you don't care. And I did. I cared about making the Pom Squad more than anything I could ever remember. "This is really terrific," I muttered to myself. "First I can't win, and now I'm not even good at losing. What kind of loser can't even work up a few tears?"

Before I had a chance to answer myself, I heard a tap on my wall. In my hurry to flop on my bed, I had forgotten to shut my door. I looked up. Standing in my doorway was my grandfather. He was wearing his most understanding smile.

Seeing him there made me feel even worse. Here the poor man had come all the way up to my room to console me, and I couldn't even manage a tear for him to wipe away. Sometimes it seemed that all I was good at was disappointing people.

"Don't think that because I'm not crying that it means I'm not upset," I muttered. "Because I am. I'm the most upset I've ever been in my life. I think

I'm just in shock or something. I'll probably fall apart any minute now."

Granddad sat down on the end of my bed and sighed thoughtfully. "There could be another explanation, you know," he said quietly. "Maybe you're not crying because way down deep inside, you know that you're not really a loser."

I hate that. Why does everybody insist on trying to make losing sound like winning? They're not even related! "Of course I'm a loser!" I snapped. "I lost, didn't I?"

Granddad didn't seem to mind being snapped at. "If you practiced hard and tried your best, you're not a loser, Lillian," he insisted gently.

I rolled my eyes. "*Please,* Granddad! I just don't think I could stand another You're Not Really a Loser speech. A loser is a person who loses. And I ought to know. I'm the biggest loser of all time."

My grandfather got a stern look on his face and stood up. "Don't you *ever* let me hear you say anything like that again," he ordered. "Because you're wrong, Lillian. You are absolutely dead wrong. A loser is *not* a person who loses. It's a lot sadder than that."

Then he turned and walked to the door. When he got there he stared at me a minute. "A loser is a

person who stops dreaming of ever being a winner."
After he shut the door behind him, I sat there looking at where he had been. A second later, I began
to cry. When your grandfather raises his voice at
you, it's different from when your mom and dad do.
For some reason, it seems more serious.

I didn't see Granddad for two weeks. I started to
call him a couple of times, but I didn't know what
I would say. Then last weekend Grandma Woo-
Woo called and invited us over. It was Granddad's
birthday, and she wanted us to help him celebrate.

When I walked up the porch to his house, Granddad hurried outside and hugged me tighter than he's
ever hugged me before. I think he wanted to be sure
I knew he wasn't mad at me. I knew.

After we had eaten his birthday dinner, Grandma
Woo-Woo brought out the presents. He opened
mine first. When he saw it, I thought he was going
to start to cry. It was only my school picture, with
I love you, Granddad, written on it. But my mom
said it would mean a lot to him, and I guess she was
right.

He opened Aunt Millie's last. It was a cane. She
sent a note saying that she knew he didn't need it
yet, but at his age, he could fall down and break
something at any minute. When Granddad saw it,

he rolled his eyes. Then, he said Aunt Millie was berserk.

Grandma Woo-Woo got mad. She snatched the cane away from him and said he didn't deserve it. I guess she's even more sensitive about Aunt Millie than my mother.

After the presents had been opened, it was time for the cake. Grandma Woo-Woo had ordered it special from the bakery. She even had them put seventy-one candles on it, so you can imagine how big it was. Before she lit them, she put a small fire extinguisher on the table next to her. She said that with that many candles, you couldn't be too careful. Granddad didn't laugh.

Finally, though, my mother turned the lights off, and my grandmother carried the lighted cake into the dining room. It was really beautiful. We all sang "Happy Birthday," and my grandfather almost cried again. Things like that mean a lot to him.

After we finished singing, he stood up and got ready to blow. But right before he did, I couldn't help noticing that he closed his eyes for a few seconds and smiled to himself. At first, I thought the candle smoke was bothering him, but then I realized what was happening. At the age of seventy-one, my granddad was still making wishes.

Just then, a special feeling came over me. I had

felt it once before. It was the day I found out I had inherited my long legs from Uncle Edward. And now I knew that I had inherited something else. . . .

I get my dreams from my grandfather. It's a special gift that I'll try to keep with me forever. And I love him for it.

Last night, Drew and I spent the night at Belinda's. The choir was holding their Spring Sing-Along in the school auditorium, and even though we had already seen it in school, we decided to go. During intermission, the eighth-grade Pom Squad performed. At the end of their routine, they tried to make a human pyramid, and one of the bottom girls collapsed. No one was hurt, but it wasn't a very pretty sight.

I'm not sure if I'll try out for anything again next year or not. If I could teach myself to do a flip over the summer, I guess I could give cheerleading a try. But being this tall, I have a feeling I'd end up looking like a Slinky. Anyway, next year's still a long way off, so I don't have to decide right now. I just wish Drew and Belinda would stop trying to hurry me into making a decision. It really seems to be driving them crazy.

"You've got to join *something*," urged Belinda

as the three of us sat on her bed talking after the Sing-Along. "It's just not natural for you to be so calm about something this important. I'm telling you, Lillian, if you don't start joining stuff in the eighth grade, you'll never prepare yourself for all the joining you have to do in high school. Brenda said that she joined six different groups in her very first year. I remember it was her first year because that was the year she stayed back."

Drew made a face. "You mean your mother actually flunked the ninth grade?"

Belinda beamed with pride and nodded. "Brenda was the only girl at Kennedy High School who was a cheerleader for five years in a row."

Quickly, Drew covered her head with her pillow. I think she was trying to keep herself from saying something mean. When she finally came up for air, she seemed to be back under control.

"I think the important thing about joining any organization is that it can help you develop your talents." Then, she got off the bed, walked over to her suitcase, and pulled her new flute out of the side pocket.

Drew's been trying to get me interested in the flute ever since she dropped out of the Pom Squad tryouts. "Isn't this a beauty?" she asked, shining it on her flannel robe. "The wonderful thing about the flute is that it doesn't get spit in it like the other wind instruments."

I didn't tell her, but just the mention of spit makes me sick.

"Even though I've only had three lessons, I already know how to play a popular tune," she continued. Then she stood there with this big grin on her face, waiting for someone to ask her to play it.

"Play it," I muttered finally. I didn't really want to hear it, but her grin was getting on my nerves.

Drew got the music from her suitcase and propped it up on Belinda's dresser. Then she wet her lips real good and started tooting.

Ten minutes later, she put it back in its case. It was the longest ten minutes of my life. Then, she sat down on the bed and made us guess what song she had played. It took a little figuring, but I finally guessed "Silent Night." Belinda said she wasn't sure of the name, but she'd heard it played at her great-uncle's funeral.

Unfortunately, it was "Rhinestone Cowboy." Drew didn't speak to either of us for thirty minutes.

While Drew pouted, Belinda began telling me about her work on the school paper. She got on the committee without much trouble, but she said they weren't too interested in her fashion-editor idea.

Even so, she's already planning to wear her hair in a bun. It's much too short in the back, so she's going to use a lot of bobby pins and glue it together with hair spray. "The back doesn't matter because you can't see it from the front," she explained.

Anyway, she said that if I wanted to join the newspaper, they're always looking for new cub reporters. I told her no thanks. The truth is, the newspaper doesn't interest me much more than the flute.

"I wish you guys would just stop worrying about me," I said finally. "I'm sure that by the time next September rolls around I'll find something to join. Just the other day in P.E., Mrs. Manly asked me if I would consider coming out for the girls' track team."

Drew stopped her silent treatment and made another face. "The track team?" she repeated, sounding disgusted. "Ick. Maybe she was just kidding."

"That's impossible," replied Belinda. "Mrs. Manly has no sense of humor."

"For your information," I said, feeling slightly offended, "Mrs. Manly told me that with the good spring I got on my jumps in tryouts, she thinks I'd be a natural at the long jump. And besides, even if I wasn't great at it, I still think it might be fun to ride the bus to all the meets and stuff. I'm not saying I'm going to do it, but at least it's a possibility."

Belinda squinted her eyes as if she was giving the matter some thought. "What do the uniforms look like?" she asked at last. "I bet I could jump pretty good myself if the uniforms were cute enough."

Drew covered her head with the pillow again.

I didn't tell them, but Mrs. Manly isn't the only teacher interested in me either. Yesterday, as I was on my way to my locker, Mrs. Knutson stopped me in the hallway. And since it was Friday, she really caught me in a good mood.

"Lillian Pinkerton!" she exclaimed. "Just the girl I was looking for. Next week I'm going to be starting a social studies unit on Indians. And since I saw how artistic you were with the Christmas decorations, I was wondering if you would be interested in helping me do some Indian drawings for my bulletin boards."

Pleased that she had thought of me as an artist, I smiled. "Sure," I joked. "Maybe I could even wrap myself in colored paper one day and come as a totem pole."

My words really took me by surprise. I hardly ever joke about myself like that, and when I heard what I was saying, I couldn't believe my ears. Neither could Mrs. Knutson. Most of my teachers think of me as the serious type. She stood there for a second smiling weakly and then walked away. "Just what the world needs," she mumbled. "Another seventh-grade comedian."

Anyway, the whole incident really had started me thinking, and it was still on my mind that night as the three of us were going to bed. Belinda had just finished brushing her hair fifty strokes. Drew was trying to wriggle into her sleeping bag which was next to mine.

"Ever make fun of yourself?" I asked casually as I helped zip her in.

Drew looked positively insulted. "What's to make fun of?"

"Nothing. Don't take it personally. It's just that I made this little joke about my height yesterday morning and—"

"You?" interrupted Drew in total disbelief. "You made a joke about your height?"

"I know. I was pretty surprised myself. Mrs. Knutson was asking me to help her with this Indian project and I told her I'd come as a totem pole."

"A totem pole?" repeated Belinda, giggling.

Drew looked even more puzzled. "It just doesn't sound like something you'd say."

"I know. But wouldn't it be funny if I really did it? Can't you just see me? It would be even better than the time I was a maypole. You know, sometimes I think my last name should have been Pole.

Just think of all the great middle names I could have: Totem . . . May . . . Bean. . . ."

"North, South," added Drew quickly.

"Fishing," said Belinda quietly, beginning to giggle.

I stopped to think for a second. "I know. How about if I worked for the phone company. Then I could be Lillian Telephone Pole."

Belinda laughed harder. "Yeah. And when you hung out the wash, you could be known as Lillian Clothes Pole."

The two of us started giggling loudly. "Wait!" yelled Drew holding her hands up to try and silence our laughter. "I've got it. You could dedicate your life to working with frogs and your middle name could be Tad. Lillian Tad Pole." She hardly had the words out of her mouth before Belinda fell off the bed holding her sides.

For a few minutes none of us could speak. Drew and I were hysterical watching Belinda roll around on the floor. Finally, she got a hold of herself, sat up, and let out a sigh.

"I tried to get my mother to change my name once but she wouldn't do it."

"What'd you want to change it to?"

"Belinda Model."

Drew and I stared at each other for a second trying not to laugh, but we just couldn't hold it in. Belinda Model sounded so stupid, I wasn't sure I'd ever be able to stop laughing again.

Drew almost started choking. "I've got one," she sputtered, trying to catch her breath. "I could be . . . I could be . . . Drew Dough-Boy."

That did it. The three of us went wild. Belinda had to run into the bathroom before she had an accident. My stomach hurt so bad I couldn't decide whether to keep laughing or start crying.

I guess we were really being noisy. After a few minutes, Mrs. Fischer appeared in the doorway and shouted, "That's enough!" It sort of took me by surprise. It was the first time I'd ever heard her yell like a normal mother.

She made us turn out the light, probably thinking it would settle us down. But even in the dark, we couldn't seem to stop giggling. In fact, when I finally went to sleep, I must have grinned all night because the next morning my lips sort of ached.

I hate to sound corny, but I think that even if I wished as hard as I could, I couldn't find two better friends than Drew and Belinda. I can't really explain it, but sometimes good friends can almost make your problems disappear for a while. Even when you're thirteen. Even when you're a beanpole. . . .

And if that's not magic, what is?

BARBARA PARK is one of the funniest and most popular children's novelists around today. Her books include *Skinnybones, The Kid in the Red Jacket, Operation: Dump the Chump,* and *Buddies.* She lives in Phoenix with her husband and two sons.

Is there a trick to finding Mr. Right?

MARCI'S SECRET BOOK OF FLIRTING
(Don't Go Out Without It!)
by Jan Gelman

Now that they're in junior high, Marci and Pam know their dating careers should be starting. What they don't know is how to *get* them started. How will they actually meet boys? They decide to ask Marci's former baby-sitter, Cathy, for advice, and she comes through with flying colors. Soon Marci and Pam are learning how to flirt—with step-by-step instructions based on Cathy's expert research. The question is, will their new technique work on Peter, the cutest hunk in the seventh grade, and his blue-eyed buddy, Dave?

FIRST TIME IN PRINT!

BULLSEYE BOOKS PUBLISHED BY ALFRED A. KNOPF, INC.

Friendship isn't always easy...

AND THE OTHER, GOLD
by Susan Wojciechowski

When eighth-grader Patty Dillman catches a football in the face, she never imagines that it will help her catch a boyfriend! But before she knows it, she and Tim—the thrower of the football (and a hunk!)—are quite an item. Patty is thrilled, and devotes her time—which used to be spent getting into trouble with her best friend, Tracy—talking to Tim, thinking about Tim, and daydreaming about Tim. So where does that leave Tracy? Patty won't even talk to Tracy on the phone because Tim might call! Feeling left out and discouraged, Tracy begins to spend time with her friends from the school play—and now Patty starts feeling rejected! Can their friendship survive the greatest challenge known to teenage girls—the boyfriend?

"Refreshing and believable." —*Publishers Weekly*

"Likable and breezy." —*School Library Journal*

"Right on target!" —*Booklist*

BULLSEYE BOOKS PUBLISHED BY ALFRED A. KNOPF, INC.

Patty Dillman's got more boy trouble in…

PATTY DILLMAN OF HOT DOG FAME
by Susan Wojciechowski

Patty Dillman is sure she's in love. She's got all the symptoms—every time she sees Tim, her hands start to sweat, her heart starts to pound, and her legs turn to jelly. But Tim doesn't seem to notice—he's too busy skiing. So, in order to keep her place in his heart, Patty decides to take ski lessons. After all, how hard can it be? But she soon learns that it's going to take more than a few quick lessons to solve her problems. Between the hours she spends volunteering at the local soup kitchen, baby-sitting to make enough money to go on a romantic ski trip with Tim, taking ski lessons, *and* trying to keep up with her schoolwork, Patty hardly knows whether she's coming or going. But one thing she *does* know is that she hasn't seen Tim for weeks—and if she's not careful, she may end up losing the love of her life!

"A spirited follow-up to the first book…breezy and entertaining." —*Publishers Weekly*

BULLSEYE BOOKS PUBLISHED BY ALFRED A. KNOPF

Why couldn't they just stay twelve forever?

THE TROUBLE WITH THIRTEEN
by Betty Miles

Annie and Rachel think life at twelve is just perfect. Even though all their friends are in such a hurry to grow up, wanting things like pierced ears and boyfriends, the two of them are happy with things the way they are. But things can't stay the same forever. First Annie's beloved dog dies in her arms. Then Rachel's parents decide to get a divorce, and that means Rachel will be moving to New York City with her mother. Annie is afraid that living in New York will turn Rachel into a stuck-up city girl, and Rachel is scared of losing her cherished position as Annie's best friend. But together Annie and Rachel learn a lot about independence and loyalty—and that there are, after all, some good things about turning thirteen.

"Authentic, balanced and believable...the book is a winner." —*School Library Journal*

"Solid gold!" —*Publishers Weekly*

BULLSEYE BOOKS PUBLISHED BY ALFRED A. KNOPF, INC.